Corra took a bite of the cake and closed her eyes. When she licked the remaining icing from her lips, he wanted to reach over and help her out.

"Mmm, this is so good, and moist." Then she took a sip of wine.

Chris did the same.

After a few minutes of talking and eating, he noticed chocolate on Corra's lip.

He leaned closer to her. "You've got something right there," he said, before licking the speck of chocolate from her bottom lip.

Corra smiled. "Did you really just do that? That was a movie move if I've ever seen one."

"Not original enough for you, huh?"

She laughed. "Not quite. Why don't you try something like this?" Corra leaned over and grabbed him by the collar. "Let's see what your cake tastes like."

The moment her mouth met his, warmth flooded his body and the desire to take her became an overpowering need. He wanted her closer.

Dear Reader,

Thank you so much for purchasing *The Only One for Me*, the second book in the Coleman House series. I hope you'll enjoy reading Corra and Christopher's story. Coleman House is a series near and dear to my heart. While riding through the countryside in Kentucky I saw this massive house that reminded me of Tara from *Gone with the Wind*. My curiosity about who lived there took over, and my own experience at a B and B fueled the rest. Running both an organic farm and a B and B is hard work. Nobody knows that better than the Colemans.

To learn more about me and future releases, please sign up for my newsletter at www.bridgetanderson.net. I love to connect with readers, so follow me on Twitter, @Banders319, or www.Facebook.com/Banders319. I appreciate all reviews. Please take the time to leave one.

Thank you,

Bridget Anderson

The Only One for
Me

Bridget Anderson

⟨H⟩ **HARLEQUIN**® KIMANI™ ROMANCE

Recycling programs
for this product may
not exist in your area.

ISBN-13: 978-0-373-86495-9

The Only One for Me

Copyright © 2017 by Bridget Anderson

For questions and comments about the quality of this book please contact us
at CustomerService@Harlequin.com.

HARLEQUIN®
™ www.Harlequin.com

Printed in U.S.A.

Bridget Anderson writes provocative stories about smart women and the men they love. She has over nine published novels and two novellas to date. Her romance suspense novel *Rendezvous* was adapted into a made-for-television movie.

When Bridget's not writing, she loves to travel. She's fallen in love with Paris, France, and can't wait to get back to Ghana, West Africa. She's a native of Louisville, Kentucky, who currently resides north of metro Atlanta with her husband and a big dog that she swears is part human.

I'd like to dedicate this book to all the hardworking bed-and-breakfast innkeepers out there. Running a bed-and-breakfast is truly a labor of love.

Chapter 1

Corra Coleman danced around her cozy kitchen preparing breakfast and lunch for her children, Jamie and Katie, while she kept a keen eye on the clock. A typical Wednesday morning at the Coleman household.

"Mom, I can't find my charm bracelet," Katie whined.

Corra finished stuffing their lunch boxes, and then pushed them to the end of the counter. "Honey, it's not in your backpack?"

"No, that's where I'm looking." Katie stood up and turned her backpack upside down, spilling the contents onto the middle of the kitchen floor.

"Katie!" Corra barked.

"Mom, can I go back upstairs and get my baseball glove?" Jamie asked from his seat at the kitchen table.

"Have you finished your cereal?" Corra asked, as she hurried over to help Katie sort through her belongings on the floor.

"Yes, ma'am."

"Okay, but hurry. The school bus will be outside any minute now, and we're already in trouble for holding up the bus."

Jamie pushed his chair back and ran for the stairs.

"It's not here." Katie started to cry.

"Well, honey, maybe it's in your room. Go on up and look for it real quick." The bracelet was a birthday present from her uncle Rollin last year. The first day she wore it to school she aced her exam and was selected as the lead in her school play. Since then, she wore her lucky charm to school every day.

Katie took off running while Corra buckled her backpack. The way she calculated it she had about twenty seconds to sip some coffee before they came stampeding back down the stairs. She never had time to eat breakfast at home. She walked over to the back door and looked out. Between the houses in back of her she could see the school bus on the next block.

She grabbed the lunch boxes and Katie's backpack and hurried to the front door. She glanced up the stairs on her way. "What are you two doing up there, the school bus is on the way."

Ten-year-old Jamie took the stairs two at a time and practically crashed into Corra on his way out.

She hollered out the door. "If you don't come

home with that glove don't come at all. I'm not buying another one."

With his backpack on one shoulder, and his glove on one hand, Jamie threw up the other hand signifying he'd heard her.

The bus pulled to a screeching halt a few houses down. Corra turned around looking for Katie. "Katie, come on, the bus is here."

"But Mom, I still can't find my bracelet."

From the bottom of the stairs Corra looked up at her baby who looked like someone had broken her heart. *Oh man, he's going to honk his horn, I know he is.* Although her leg was nearly healed after being broken in an accident seven months ago, Corra still wasn't up to jogging up the stairs. She'd just have to deal with the bus driver because she had to help her baby.

Once upstairs in Katie's room, she started tossing clothes and covers around. "Where did you last see it?" she asked.

"It was on the dresser when I went to bed last night."

Corra walked over and peered behind the dresser, and there lay Katie's bracelet, and a few other items. Corra pulled the dresser out a little. "Bingo." She retrieved everything, and handed Katie the bracelet. Alongside of the bracelet was a small baby picture of Katie and her father, Eric Hayden, during happier times. Corra hadn't seen this picture in a long time, or her ex in over two years.

The school bus horn sounded and Corra slapped

the picture facedown on the dresser. If she didn't see that again it would be too soon.

"Come on, young lady." She grabbed Katie's hand and hurried out of the room. Katie trotted down the stairs ahead of her.

Katie pulled on her jacket and her backpack, and then gave Corra a hug and a kiss before she ran out the door. Corra stood on the porch and waved as the bus passed. There went the two most important people in her life.

Thirty minutes later, Corra was in her car listening to the radio as she hurried down the quiet picturesque two-lane road that led to her family's business. The Coleman House bed-and-breakfast was not only her parents' legacy to her and her brother Rollin, it was also now her place of employment. She pulled her car around the back of the new gift shop into her reserved spot and climbed out.

She walked across the driveway to the back of the house. From outside she could smell the coffee, and breakfast that Rita prepared for the guests that morning. She knocked before opening the back door, then walked in.

"Morning, Corra, grab yourself a plate before I put everything away." Rita Coleman, Corra's aunt by marriage and the bed-and-breakfast's head cook, housekeeper and master gardener came over and planted her usual kiss on Corra's cheek.

"Morning, Rita." Corra put her purse in the back hall closet and returned to grab herself a plate.

"Everybody's out this morning doing one thing or another, but the truck will be back soon and I want to get the kitchen cleaned up."

Corra looked up at the clock on the kitchen wall. It was almost nine o'clock, which meant she had thirty minutes to eat before she prepared to open the gift shop. "I'm pressed for time this morning too." Corra sat at the small kitchen table. "I've got a local artist bringing some things for consignment."

"I didn't know you did consignments?" Rita said, as she poured Corra a cup of coffee.

"We just started. One of Tayler's ideas." Her soon-to-be sister-in-law, Tayler Carter, left her job in Chicago to be with Rollin, and brought a wealth of business-building ideas with her.

After Corra finished her breakfast the back door swung open and her older brother, Rollin, walked in. She hadn't expected to see him since most of his mornings were spent out on the farm.

Dressed in his usual jeans, cotton T-shirt and boots, he walked in wiping his forehead with the back of his hand. "Morning Rollin, I thought you were already out checking the crops by now," Corra said.

"I was, but I've got some business to take care of in town. Some of us start work before 8:00 a.m., missy." He grabbed a glass from the cabinet and walked over to the refrigerator for water.

"Rollin, you know I can't get here any earlier. I have to get the kids off to school." He teased her about her hours every week. Since she quit managing Save-A-Lot groceries and started working at the Coleman House she'd only averaged about thirty hours a week.

Rollin threw back his water and set the glass on the counter. "Sis, I need you to do something for me today."

"What's that?" Corra asked, as she finished her plate and pushed it aside.

"I'm expecting a guy to drop by this morning and demo a new computer program. I need you to handle it for me."

"Me! Why me? You know more about that system than I do. Or Tayler, she knows it."

"Tayler's in town taking care of some business and there's an issue with the last shipment for Whole Foods that I need to attend to. You can do it. Just see if what he has is better than what we're currently using."

"But, I have a client coming by this morning." She placed her plate and his glass in the dishwasher.

"He's not coming until around noon. And it won't take long." Rollin turned and looked out the back window. "Here comes the morning truck. You should have seen the crew this morning. They're from the city and were so excited to tour the farm they practically ran out and jumped on the truck."

Corra walked over to the window and stood beside her brother. The pickup truck slowly made its way up the road to the house. The bed-and-breakfast was a working farm where every morning at 8:00 a.m. Kevin, a full-time employee, and Kyla, their cousin and a new employee, loaded the guests on the back of the truck and carried them out to the fields to pick the day's meal. Rita would prepare their vegetables and fruits for dinner. However, nothing was in season at the moment. So, the guests toured the farm.

"We've got a full house this week, don't we?" Corra asked.

"Yep. For Greek Alumni week at the college, Tayler suggested we offer a discount. Booked us up for two weeks. After that we have a few vacancies."

"Well, I'd better get ready to open the gift shop."

"Hey, don't forget about the computer guy. He'll come to the house, not the gift shop."

"Rollin, how can I be in two places at once?"

"Kyla will help you out. Let her cover the shop once he gets here."

Corra nodded. In the time Corra spent recovering from a broken fibula, Tayler had convinced Rollin to do something she couldn't—hire more staff. Tayler had taken over serving breakfast from Rollin while Rita remained the queen of the kitchen. To assist her they'd brought on two relatives. Tracee Coleman, who'd spent five years working for a bakery in Louisville, Kentucky, and her younger sister Kyla who was working on her Ph.D. in Agricultural Economics from the University of Kentucky. She worked on the farm four days a week. She had even helped Rollin set up an internship with the local college. They currently had two young interns onboard.

Corra walked outside as the truck pulled up. She waved to Kevin as Kyla jumped off the back of the

truck. She gave a few instructions to the guests before waving at Corra.

"Morning, Corra. You missed a fun ride this
morning."

"I'm sure I did." Corra waved back. Kyla had the
body of a dancer, with her long legs and trim figure.
She was super smart, highly adaptable, and she had
an insatiable curiosity about the bed-and-breakfast.
She was just the type of employee they needed.

Seconds after Corra opened up shop the bell over
the door jingled. In walked her first customer of the
day.

When the decision was made to move 3C Evolution's call center to Danville, Kentucky, two em-
ployees accepted the offer to move with Christopher
Williams. Customer service manager Terry Davis
and office manager Valerie Amares were now Danville residents.

The new office was small, but large enough to
cover the Southeastern territory. Chris and Terry
walked out of a meeting where they discussed how
successfully the staffing of the center was going.

"Chris, are you sure you don't want me to handle
this demo for you?" Terry asked.

"I can handle this one. The bed-and-breakfast is
owned by one of my former teammates."

"The Coleman House?" Terry asked.

"Yeah, Rollin Coleman and I played football together in high school. We had some great times out
at the farm. Some of which I can't tell you about."

Terry laughed. "Yeah, I bet. Getting girls in the cornfield."

Chris shrugged. "Hey, don't knock it."

"Naw, man. I understand. I grew up in a small town myself outside of Indianapolis. I was on my high school basketball team. It was by far the best time of my life. But, those were the good old days," Terry concluded.

Terry walked down the hall with Chris until they stood at Val's desk.

"Headed out, Chris?" Val asked.

"I'm going to swing by my folks' place first, then I'll be at the Coleman House if anybody's looking for me."

"We'll hold the fort down," Terry said.

"Do you think you'll be back in time for the four o'clock conference call?" Val asked.

Chris snapped his fingers. "I forgot all about that." He turned to Terry. "What are you doing at four o'clock?"

Terry's eyes widened. "Uh, nothing."

"Great." Chris turned to Val. "Terry will sit in for me. Let Craig know."

"But it's a director's meeting!" Terry's voice rose.

"Good preparation for the increased responsibilities you'll have here. Just keep me abreast of what's going on."

Chris laughed at the startled looks on Terry and Val's faces. He had a promotion in mind for the both of them, as long as the call center went off without a hitch.

Chris suddenly thought of Corra Coleman. He'd been in town two weeks and he hadn't seen or spoken to her since his return. Although he'd been extremely busy getting everything functional and assisting Terry in hiring a supervisor and a few call center reps, he should have called Corra the day he arrived. The last time he spoke to her she was recovering nicely from the accident and had no hard feelings toward him. He hoped those emotions hadn't changed.

Chapter 2

Seven years ago, Chris sold his first business and purchased his parents a modest home on Mitchellsburg Road. The ranch-style home sat on four acres, and was big enough for family barbecues, yet small enough for his mother to get around without much help.

Chris pulled his Cadillac CT6 all the way up to the garage door and killed the engine. Since his return to Danville two weeks ago he'd only visited his parents once, and hadn't seen his little sister, Pamela, at all. All of that was about to change. Pamela's car was parked next to his.

Chris climbed out of the car and walked around to the front door. He rang the bell and waited for his father to answer. Instead, Pamela threw the door open.

"Hey, big bro, it's good to see you." Pamela stood on her tiptoes to greet Chris with a hug.

Chris squeezed her so hard he lifted her off the ground.

"Chris." She hit him on the back. "Put me down."

After a quick kiss on the cheek he planted her feet back on the floor and released her. "Damn, you are skinnier than you were the last time I saw you. What you trying to do, waste away?"

She stepped back and stuck a pose. "I'm not skinny, I'm trim."

"Oh, yeah. Looks like you're headed toward an eating disorder to me. You're not throwing your food up, are you?"

She whacked him good on the arm. "That's not funny. Eating disorders are a disease."

"I know. I'm sorry. Come here and give me another hug."

This time he left her feet on the ground. "I think you felt a little heavier that time," he said when he released her.

"Boy." Pamela shoved him and turned away. "Mama's in the den and Daddy's out in the garage working on something."

Chris followed Pamela back into the house. His mother sat on her favorite massage lounger with a throw over her legs, looking as regal as ever. To the naked eye Dakota Williams looked fine. Since Chris was a little boy, pain had been her constant companion. Her invisible illness hadn't been easy to explain to anyone outside the family. But, after years of suffering, the final diagnosis was fibromyalgia.

"Hey Mom, how you doing?" He bent over and kissed his mother on the forehead before giving her one of his bear hugs. His heart swelled every time he saw his mother.

"I'm fine, baby. And happy to see you."

"How's the pain today?" he asked.

"Oh, it's about a six. That's why I'm sitting down here watching all these talk shows with Pamela." She glanced up at Chris. "You know personally I'd rather read a book."

Pamela crossed her arms. "I thought you wanted to watch *The View*?"

"I do, honey. *The View* or whatever that other show was you had me watching a few minutes ago. I tell you, I don't see how those women have the energy to keep trying to outtalk each other every day."

Chris chuckled and planted himself on the edge of his mother's lounger. "If your pain gets up to an eight, you have Pamela help you to bed."

"Honey, I'm okay. I swear, you worry about me more than I stress about myself."

"I just want to make sure you're comfortable is all."

"I couldn't be more comfortable than in this massager. Thank you again for the chair, it helps so much."

"I'm glad. The minute I saw it I thought about you." Chris looked at Pamela who was so engrossed in her talk show he doubted she remembered he was in the room.

"I'm going out to the garage and see what Daddy's up to." He gave his mother another kiss on the forehead.

"I hope he's not working on another table out there. We've got enough already."

Chris walked down the hall lined with family pictures from his childhood to the present. He opened the door to the garage and could hear his father's radio playing quietly in the corner while he tinkered with another creation. When Chris closed the door, his father turned around.

"How's everything, Chris? Glad you stopped by. Let me get your opinion on something."

"Sure, what you up to?" Chris walked over to see what his father was taking apart now. Before Nathaniel Williams's former employer up and left Danville, he had a very stressful career. Between work and taking care of his wife he needed an outlet, so he took up woodworking. Now Chris's dad was one of the most sought-after table designers and furniture repairmen in the county. His original and custom pieces had been commissioned from as far away as the Caribbean Islands.

When Chris was young he used to help his dad build things for work, and remodel their home. Once he started playing football, he spent his summers working in construction for extra money. Between the two of them, they could build a house. And that's exactly what Chris planned on doing.

Chris placed his hand on his father's shoulder and observed the handcrafted cigar box he worked on. His father was an inch shorter than Chris's six-two frame, and thinner too.

"Which one of those designs do you like?" Nathaniel asked, pointing to a piece of paper next to the box. "Mr. Richardson up the street commissioned me to create a set of cigar boxes for his boys about to go off to college."

Chris frowned. "They smoke cigars?"

"I reckon not. He just wanted all of them to have something special from him."

Chris picked up the paper and read the inscription written in two different fonts. "I like the second one. It's fancy, but still legible."

His father took the paper from him. "Perfect. That's what I hoped you'd say. That's my choice as well." With the paper he tapped Chris softly upside his head. "Like I always say, two heads are better than one."

"Or, great minds think alike. Don't forget that one," Chris added.

Nathaniel laughed. "So what brings you by so early? Your day's not over already, is it?"

Chris walked over and balanced himself on a stool near the radio. "I'm on my way out to the Colemans' to demo some new software. I had a few minutes to spare so I thought I'd drop by."

"That's your friend Rollin's place, right?"

"Yes sir."

"Umm-hum." Nathaniel picked up the box and

examined his handiwork. "Isn't he the one whose sister was in the car with you when you totaled it last year?"

Chris usually kept his dates to himself, but everyone in town probably knew about that accident. "Yep, that's him."

"What's his sister's name?"

"Corra."

"Yeah, I've seen her around. She's the manager over at Save-A-Lot, isn't she? Or she used to be. Haven't seen her around lately."

His father did a lot of the grocery shopping for the family and he'd probably run into Corra on several occasions.

"Have you?" Nathaniel asked.

Chris shook his head. "No. I haven't seen her since I've been back."

"Why not?" Nathaniel asked, as he put the box down and cleaned up his work area.

Chris shrugged. "Haven't had time. Opening the call center is a lot of work. Besides, I'm probably the last person she wants to see."

"I thought you said you were on good terms with her when you left town?"

"Yeah I was. We even talked on the phone a couple of times after I left, but then I got busy and she never called me back. I haven't spoken to her in months."

"Son, I know you feel bad about the accident, but it wasn't your fault."

"I know. But if only I'd let her ride with her friends instead, it might not have happened."

"Or, the drunk driver might have hit them and the accident could have been much worse. You can't play what-if, or place blame anywhere other than on the drunk driver."

"I hear you, but it's still hard not to feel responsible. Especially when I wasn't hurt, and she could have been killed."

"Look at it this way. At least you two have something in common."

Chris stood up laughing. "Yeah, that's one way of looking at it." He followed his father back inside the house.

Once Chris had his father, mother and Pamela in the den together he decided to spring the good news on them.

"If you guys have a second I'd like to fill you in on something," he said, as he sat in one of the side chairs next to the couch.

His father had washed his hands and took his place in his favorite chair opposite his wife's. Pamela lay across the couch, still heavily engrossed in some television show.

"Sure, what is it?" His mother readjusted herself on the lounger.

Chris clasped his hands together. "Remember the old Whitfield place?"

"Of course. James Whitfield used to be the richest man in the county. That property has a helicopter landing pad out back for when he'd fly back and forth to Louisville. That was back in his heyday before they had to shut the plant down." Nathaniel crossed his legs, ready to go down memory lane. "I used to make a delivery up there a couple times a year. You might not remember, Chris, but I used to take you with me."

"Yeah, I remember going up there. I also remember peering out the window every day as the school bus passed the property. In the winter after the leaves fell from the trees you could see the house pretty good. I always said one day I was going to own that house."

Pamela sat up on the couch, fully at attention now. "No, you didn't!" she said.

"Chris, you bought that old place?" his mother asked.

Chris nodded. "Yes, I did." He looked at his father who was sitting back in his chair, and thought about how hard he had worked for the Whitfields all his life and never got as far as the entryway of that house.

Nathaniel smiled from ear to ear. "Son, I'm proud of you. You've really made some strides in this town."

Chris smiled and hoped his accomplishments would impress a certain woman who now weighed heavily on his mind.

Chapter 3

"I can't believe we sold every single tote with the state emblem embossed on it." Corra pointed to the empty display.

"You don't have any more in the back?" Kyla asked.

"No, I thought I had enough to get us through the month. But with the Kentucky Derby coming up, I guess I underestimated. I need to order more, quick." She moved the display around, highlighting other bags.

"Mrs. Rita sent me over here to remind you about the sales guy coming at noon."

Corra looked at her watch. "Thanks, I forgot all about that."

"Yeah, she figured as much. She said you'd be at

the front desk by now if you'd remembered. Tayler's not back yet, and Tracee had car trouble this morning, so I'm helping out with lunch today. Got a full house." Kyla turned to leave.

"Oh, Kyla, let me ask you something. Did Rollin say where he was going?"

"Nope."

"Okay, normally any time Rollin and Tayler are gone, they're usually together. Do you know where she went to this morning?"

"Nope. Rollin just said she had some business in town. Why? You think they're planning on eloping?"

The excitement in Kyla's eyes made Corra laugh. "Of course not. They wouldn't do that to us. I'm just curious about where they went to, that's all. Tell Rita I'm on my way over. I'll close the shop for a little while."

As Corra closed up she rethought the idea of Rollin eloping, but quickly dismissed the notion. He wouldn't deprive her of the joy of watching them take their vows. She only wished her parents were alive to witness the ceremony. Her own courthouse ceremony was not a proper wedding in her opinion. This one they would do up right. She locked the door and hurried over to the house.

The dining room was abuzz with all the guests fixing their plates and discussing this morning's events. Corra smiled and continued walking until she reached the private quarters of the house. In the office, she kept a pair of high heels she changed into when she worked the front desk. After a quick bathroom check of her makeup, she walked out and took her place behind the counter. She sat on a stool and turned on the computer. First, she answered a few emails, then logged into the program they used to manage guest check-in. Although she didn't use the program every day, she knew how to use it. She quickly familiarized herself with what she could.

The front door slowly opened and Corra rose. The Coleman House might be small in comparison to other bed-and-breakfasts in the area, but they were known for their first-class hospitality, which had paid off in repeat business and referrals. She'd treat this sales guy like a potential customer.

When the door opened all the way and Christopher Williams stepped in, Corra almost fell backward off her stool. She hadn't seen Chris since his last visit to her hospital room seven months and three weeks ago, to be exact. Afterward he called her a couple of times, but kept the conversations brief.

He closed the door and glanced around the entrance, smiling, before he noticed first the front desk, and then Corra. The look on his face was priceless. She crossed her arms and couldn't hold back the sarcasm.

"Well, look what the cat dragged in."

He recovered quickly and ran a hand over his mouth. "Corra, I didn't expect to see you here," he said, as he approached the front desk.

"Same here." She tried to hold on to her sarcasm although she wanted to grin from ear to ear. Chris was a six-foot-two-inch, two-hundred-and-something-pound precision-honed man who looked like he could pick up a football today and get back in the game. He was still as handsome as ever. He locked his grayish-brown eyes on her as he crossed the floor, giving her a big smile. Her heartbeat raced.

"I'm scheduled to meet Rollin at noon. But I have a feeling he's not here."

She rose from the stool. "Nope. I'm your man, or woman. Whatever you planned to show him, you can now show me."

Chris jerked his head back. "This is you?" he asked, pointing at the front desk.

She nodded.

"What happened, the grocery story wouldn't take you back after you recovered?"

"Oh, they took me back. Then I quit. I promised Rollin if he didn't close down the bed-and-breakfast I would join the staff and work to grow the business."

Chris set his laptop case down and applauded. "Smart choice. If you can run a grocery store you can run any establishment."

Corra rubbed her palms along the counter. "Well, I'm not actually running things, yet anyway, but I've learned a lot."

Chris took a step back and widened his stance. "So my business meeting is with you?"

"Yes sir. And if it's okay with you can we work right here?"

"Sure." Chris picked up his case and pulled out his laptop.

Corra welcomed him to have a seat behind the

counter. She pulled up another stool and they sat side by side while he showed her how he could improve their everyday lives with a simple program.

"Our system is cloud based, so you can access it from anywhere on any device." He pulled the program up on his computer and Corra's initial reaction was to move her head closer to the screen and raise one brow.

"Don't worry, it's a very approachable, intuitive interface that I can teach you."

She sat up. "Let's get started."

In a little over an hour Chris gave Corra a demo of the system and had his first beta customer. She just had to clear things with Rollin and they would be installing the new test system within the week.

"See, that was painless, wasn't it?" Chris asked, as he closed out the program.

Corra sat back, clasped her hands together and stretched her arms out in front of her. "No, that wasn't bad at all. Not only does it help with online booking, but I like that it helps us maintain the gift shop, the farm and anything else we want to add on. I can't believe Rollin wasn't already using something like this."

Chris crossed his arms. "Neither can I. Trust me, after you get a chance to experience the software, you'll want this installed right away."

"Okay, I'll go over everything with Rollin and let you know what he says. But, I can't imagine him saying no, at least to a beta test after I tell him how robust the system is."

"Thank you. And if he needs a little convincing don't hesitate to call me." Chris reached into his shirt pocket and pulled out a business card. "Here's my new information."

Corra read the card. "3C Evolution has a Danville address." She tilted her head and stared up at him.

"I moved back two weeks ago and opened our customer service center here. I'm surprised you didn't read about it in the business section of the paper."

Corra almost fell off her stool. "I must have missed it. So you're here permanently now?"

"I don't know about permanently, but I'll be living here for quite a while. I've made Danville my home again."

"I bet your parents are happy?" *Not to mention how delighted I'm feeling right now.*

"They are."

"What about you? After living away for so long how do you feel about being back here?"

"It was my choice to move the center to Danville. I was ready to come home."

Corra found it hard to believe he left Philly for Danville. But deep down she knew Chris was a country boy just like Rollin. She rubbed her palms down her pants legs. "Well, I guess I should say, welcome home." She offered her hand to him.

"Thank you." He accepted her handshake.

A warm current shot up Corra's arm, reminding her of how much Chris excited her. She pursed her lips and fought the urge to blush.

"I haven't been inside this house in a long time,"

Chris said as he closed his laptop and slid it back into his carrying case.

"Would you like a quick tour?" she asked.

"That would be nice. Is Mrs. Rita still here?"

"Of course. Come on, we'll start with the kitchen."

As they toured the property fond memories of a young Corra were coming back to Chris.

"Man, I remember taking these steps two at a time," he said, as he ran his hand along the banister coming from the second floor. "Do you remember how Rollin used to chase you out of his room whenever he had a girl on the phone?"

Corra laughed. "Yes, because I was always listening at the door."

"You were being a nosy little sister is what you were doing."

"Hey, that's what I did best. Shoot, imagine what it was like for me to have football players in the house all the time. My friends came over just so they could watch you all practice in the field. That alone made me very popular in school."

"Yeah, and what about the time you brought Belinda over here when you knew Rollin had another girl down by the creek. Is that creek still there?" he asked.

Corra shook her head. "It dried up years ago. Rollin deserved that though. I never did like a two-timing man and that's what Rollin was trying to do to Belinda."

"He was young. But, man, you were a pistol growing up, you know that?"

"I was your typical little sister, no more no less."

Chris laughed. "Yeah, I guess you were, because Pamela and Darlene used to give me a hard way to go as well."

After a tour of the house Corra carried Chris over to the gift shop.

"This place is really growing. I know your parents would be proud."

"Do you remember my parents?" Corra asked, as she leaned against the counter. Her parents were killed by a drunk driver after Rollin and Chris went off to college, but she hoped he hadn't forgotten them.

"Sure. I remember your mother used to feed us after games, even when we practiced out in the field. She loved to cook, didn't she?"

Corra smiled. "The kitchen was her domain."

"And your dad came to every football game. I remember that vividly because my dad missed a lot of games when my mom was sick. Your dad was a serious football fan."

"Yeah. He was so proud when Rollin got that football scholarship."

Chris walked over and stood next to Corra. "I also remember your brother and father giving me hell in high school when I mentioned how cute you were. I wanted to ask you out, but they were very protective of you."

Corra stared down at her feet before looking up at him. "Maybe you should have tried," she suggested.

He chuckled. "At the risk of ending my friendship with Rollin, and having your father kick my ass. No thanks. I settled for admiring you from afar."

She tilted her head and bit her bottom lip. "Too bad I didn't know."

"Yeah, what would you have done?" he asked, fighting the urge to lean over and kiss her lips.

The bell over the door jingled and Corra sprang from the counter holding a hand over her heart. Two middle-aged women dressed in comfortable jogging suits and sneakers walked in.

"Customers. I'll be right back." She excused herself, and saw to her guests while Chris browsed about the store. It took the women quite some time to settle on their gifts while telling Corra all about their Greek Alumni reunion. Corra was in her element as she listened to their stories and helped them pick out suitable gifts.

After the ladies left, Chris walked back up to the counter. Corra came from behind the register.

"So where were we?" she asked.

"We were about to pick up from seven months ago when I walked into the fund-raiser and saw one of the most beautiful women in Danville. How about that date now?"

"Can I trust you to get me someplace safely this time?"

"I promise. So what are you doing tomorrow night?"

Corra smiled. "Looks like I'm going out with you."

Chapter 4

Corra had reopened the gift shop by the time Rollin and Tayler pulled up separately out front. She walked over and leaned against the door frame with her arms crossed waiting for them to exit the car.

Rollin tried to offer a nonchalant expression as he stepped out of the car. But Corra knew his mask when she saw it. Tayler, on the other hand, didn't even try to hide the big smile on her face.

"How'd it go?" Rollin asked, as they approached.

Corra decided to have a little fun. "He didn't show."

Rollin frowned. "He didn't?"

Corra shook her head. "Nope, I waited at the front desk until after one, and then I had to reopen the shop."

Rollin and Tayler glanced at one another before shrugging. "I wonder what happened," Rollin said.

"Me too," Tayler added.

"You never told me who to expect anyway. What's his name?" Corra asked. She tried to look as unconcerned as Rollin.

"A guy from 3C Evolution," Rollin said.

"Isn't that Chris's company?" she asked.

Rollin and Tayler glanced at one another, again. "Yeah, I believe it is," he said.

Corra reached inside the door and grabbed a plush toy and threw it at Rollin. "You knew Chris was coming by here. You set me up."

Rollin ducked, and Tayler laughed. "So he did come by?" she asked.

Corra went to retrieve her toy, and punched Rollin in the arm. "Yes, he was here. I think I surprised him too. Seems like no one told him I was working here."

Rollin threw his hands up. "Hey, I had every intention of meeting with him, but something came up. I'm glad you two got to talk. Did he tell you he's moved back?"

"Of course. He even asked me out."

Rollin smiled and nodded. "Well, looks like my work here is done. I'll leave you ladies to gossip about the details, I've got work to do."

Rollin left them and walked toward the house.

"You knew he was coming, didn't you?" Corra asked Tayler.

"Of course. Why do you think I made myself scarce all morning?" Tayler asked.

"For a split second I thought you and Rollin had eloped."

Tayler shook her head. "Girl, I'm sure that would be okay with Rollin, but not me. I want a wedding, and I want it right here at the Coleman House."

Corra placed her hands on her hips. "What happened to the church wedding?"

"Rollin and I talked it over. I love your church and your pastor, but I don't know a lot of people in Danville outside of the family. So, I thought a more intimate wedding right here at home would be more fitting. With your pastor officiating of course."

Corra couldn't believe her ears. "Wow, you are definitely not the same woman who came to stay here eight months ago. That woman would have wanted a big church wedding with all the bells and whistles." It seemed like years ago when Tayler checked in as a guest, and departed as Rollin's fiancée.

"Not actually. I already have what I want—Rollin. A wedding is just icing on the cake. Which reminds me of something." Tayler pulled several brochures from her huge designer purse. "When you close shop come on over to the house. I have something I need your help with."

"Business is slow, so I'll come over now." Corra put up the Back in Thirty Minutes sign. She followed Tayler over to the house. They used the back entrance since guests were sitting in the big rocking chairs on the front porch.

The minute Corra walked into the family room Rollin said, "Corra, I forgot to ask, how did the demo go?"

"Oh, it was great. That software encompasses everything we do on a daily basis and then some. He's also looking for a beta tester and I told him we'd be glad to help him out." She took a seat on the couch.

"Humph!" Tayler grunted from the other end of the couch. "Who's helping who? I told Rollin that antiquated system of his needs to be updated."

"New software is on my list of things to do. That's why I told Chris to come on by. Corra, you're practically up to speed on how the place runs, so the decision's yours. I'm putting you in charge."

"Does that mean I get a raise?" Corra asked.

"Prove you can handle some additional responsibilities and I'll see what I can do."

Corra's heart swelled. She knew eventually her brother would give her more decision-making authority. After all, the bed-and-breakfast did belong to the both of them. "In that case, I'm gonna need you to babysit your niece and nephew tomorrow night since I can't afford a babysitter."

"We'd be happy to," Tayler said.

Rollin shrugged. "Whatever she says." Then he left the room.

Tayler pulled the brochures from her purse, and scattered them over the coffee table.

Corra moved closer. "What's this?"

"Well, Rollin and I finally settled on a date. The second Saturday in July we're getting married right here."

Corra stood up and reached over to give Tayler a

big hug. "Great! I'm so happy for you two. Are you sure we don't have guests that weekend?"

"I'm positive. We blocked that weekend months ago, just in case. And I want to ask you if you'll be my maid of honor?"

Corra reached out and hugged Tayler again. "Of course I will." At this moment, she wished her mother was here.

"Nicole will be my bridesmaid, and my family's coming."

"I'm so excited. It's going to be a family affair." Corra's cousin and Tayler's best friend, Nicole, was the reason Tayler had chosen their bed-and-breakfast as a vacation spot in the first place.

Corra grabbed a brochure. "Well, let's take a look at what you've got here."

Tayler reached out and stopped her. "First, I want to hear all about Chris's visit. Did you pick up where you left off seven months ago? And where has he been since then?"

Corra took a deep breath and crossed her arms. "Well, when he walked through the door I got the shock of my life. He's the last person I expected to see, and I believe the feeling was mutual. Where has he been for the last seven months? I don't know, but I plan to find out tomorrow night."

Although Chris knew where Corra lived, she'd asked him to pick her up Friday evening at the Coleman House. He'd planned to take her to his favorite restaurant in Lexington which was about forty-five minutes away.

When he arrived the gift shop had a Closed sign on the door. He parked and headed over to the house. He didn't get too far when the door to the gift shop opened. Corra walked out, so he turned around.

"I thought I'd wait for you here. It's kind of busy in the house right now. Full house."

"Sure." Chris couldn't hold back the smile on his face. Corra had on a dress that hugged her hips and heels that showed off her beautiful legs. Her shoulder-length hair had that sexy, tousled, "I just climbed out of bed after a night of lovemaking" look. He loved it.

They met up as he walked back to the car.

"Why are you smiling?" she asked.

"I'm admiring how good you look. Your hair's different." She reached up and ran a hand through her tresses. The simple movement turned him on.

"I just thought I'd curl it for once."

He opened the car door for her.

"So, where are we headed?"

"I hope you're hungry? I'm taking you to my favorite restaurant." She eased down then swiveled ever so gently into the seat. *Damn!* She looked so inviting tonight.

"I'm famished."

He closed her door, and then walked around to the driver's side and got in.

Corra buckled herself in as he started the car.

"Is this yours?" she asked.

"Yep. This time I decided on a Made in America, Cadillac."

Corra looked around. "It's a beautiful car. I've never rode in one before. What model is this?"

"It's a CT6. If you've never had the pleasure, sit back and be prepared to be amazed." Chris turned the radio on to a soft jazz station.

"So, what did Rollin say when you explained the software to him?" Chris asked, as they pulled away from the property.

"He said it's up to me. Since I started, Tayler and I have been doing most of the administrative work, which has freed up Rollin to expand on the farm."

"That's great. I like to see families keeping business all in the family when they can. That's how you grow a legacy. Who knows, one day one of your children will be running things."

Corra laughed. "Well, I certainly hope so. That place meant a lot to my parents. That's why I couldn't let Rollin close it down. Now we're on the upswing and I only wish it was bigger."

"Expand. You have room in the back of the house to add on, don't you?"

Corra lowered her head, then gazed up at Chris. "You know Rollin. That will never happen. He's more interested in expanding the farm than the house. Which is okay with me. Either one equals more revenue at the rate we're going."

"I'm glad to hear that things are going so well. I know Rollin was concerned for a little while there. Our new management system should cut your work in half. If it doesn't let me know and I'll pay to install something else for you."

Corra snorted. "You're giving that type of a guarantee?"

"Yes ma'am. I know my product. It's damned good."

"Well, Tayler and I will be the judge of that. She's eager to get her hands on it as well."

"And I'm equally eager for you to get your hands all over it, then let me know what you think." Chris glanced over at Corra's dress as it rose up her thighs, causing a shortness in his breath. He turned his attention back to the road as they entered the expressway and he put his new automobile to the test.

It took forty-five minutes to get to Tony's Steaks and Seafood. Corra had heard of the restaurant, but had never been.

They had a huge menu selection, so it took Corra a while to decide on her entrée. The freedom of being able to pick whatever she wanted without placing another order for the kids was new to her. She hadn't been out on a date in forever and relished this experience.

She quickly placed her order, anxious for the waiter to disappear. She'd been holding something in from the minute Chris entered the bed-and-breakfast. This evening, she had to have an answer.

"So Chris, where have you been for the last seven months?"

Chapter 5

Chris lowered his gaze and took a deep breath. He'd been waiting for that question.

He smiled up at Corra. "I know I owe you an apology. I had every intention of keeping in contact. But the minute my plane landed in Philly, the chaos ensued. I had building problems, people issues, and a few other things that come with growing pains. We're opening a new office in London, so I had to make a trip there. They were good problems to have, but very time-consuming. Can you forgive me?"

He bit his bottom lip and pressed his palms together at his chest. Corra tilted her head and gave him her side eye "what do you take me for?" look.

She threw her chin up. "I'll think about it. But,

maybe we should keep things strictly business for now."

He lowered his hands and nodded. Just as he did, the waiter appeared with a bottle of champagne and two glasses. Corra gave the waiter a double take. They hadn't ordered champagne. Chris stared across the table at her while the waiter poured two glasses and complimented Chris on his selection. Corra crossed her arms as she realized he'd ordered the champagne before they arrived.

Chris picked up his glass and motioned for her to do the same. She complied. "What are we drinking to?" she asked.

"To new beginnings. The start of something beautiful. Whatever you want to call it as long as you'll forgive me." He held his glass out waiting for her to toast.

Corra set her glass down.

"So, you think this fancy restaurant and that bottle of champagne makes up for that flimsy excuse?"

Chris lowered his glass and nodded. "You're right," he said, before looking up at her. "That's not good enough. I was wrong not to communicate with you, and I hope you'll find it in your heart to forgive me. It wasn't my intention to invite you out to upset you. I want to make up for my absence, if you'll let me?"

The waiter returned with dinner, and to check on the champagne. He offered to bring out a different brand if they didn't like the first choice.

Chris smiled. "No, it's fine." He picked his glass up and held it out to Corra.

The waiter slowly backed away. She left him hanging for a few seconds before she picked her glass up again.

"To forgiveness, and new beginnings," Chris said.

Corra chuckled. "To new beginnings. You have to work for forgiveness."

Chris held his glass up higher and smiled. "That I can do."

Over dinner they discussed Chris's company and their new line of software. Corra stated she was proud of him and all of his accomplishments. The conversation moved from work to family as Corra bragged about her babies.

"Katie's my little soft-spoken princess. She's so sensitive for an eight-year-old, and I have no idea where she gets that from. Jamie, he's ten, and playing baseball this year. He's actually pretty good. If only I could stop him from losing his gloves. We're on the third one."

Chris laughed. "I'm surprised you don't have him in peewee football. The skill might run in the family."

"Oh, no. Not my son. I don't want him to play football. It's such a dangerous sport."

"Like he can't get hit with a baseball?"

Corra shrugged. "I know. But with all the controversy about concussions and football players I'm playing it safe. Besides, he doesn't have an interest."

"Then he takes after his father. Eric was good at

baseball too. He just wasn't disciplined enough to play on the team."

That was the first time Chris had ever made reference to her ex-husband, and his high school nemesis.

"I'm sorry. I didn't mean to go there."

Corra's face grew solemn. "Yes, let's not go there."

"Woo-hoo! Come on, Jamie!" Corra cheered, then bit her bottom lip as her baby stepped up to bat.

"Attaboy, Jamie!" Rollin's deep throaty cheer could be heard above all the parents in attendance. He stood and clapped so hard it hurt Corra's hands.

She held her breath as Jamie swung at the ball.

"Strike."

Rollin continued to clap. "That's okay, we'll get the next one. Focus on the ball. Come on."

"Strike two."

Oh, no. Corra crossed her legs and glanced over at Tayler and Katie who sat on the edge of their seats as they cheered Jamie on. His Sunday afternoon games had become a family affair, and Rollin hadn't missed one yet.

Jamie tapped his bat against the base before getting into his squat, serious about the next pitch. Corra crossed her fingers.

The crack of the bat sent Corra to her feet screaming with joy as her baby took off running for first base. The sight of his little legs moving so fast brought tears to her eyes.

"Run, Jamie, run!" Rollin yelled at the top of his lungs.

"Run!" everyone screamed.

When Jamie slid in for a home run Corra just about lost her mind. Being the proud mama she was, she yelled out. "That's my baby right there." Before the game was over Jamie scored two more home runs.

After they won the game, the coach pulled all the boys and their fathers together for a photo. Rollin quickly ran down the benches to take a picture with Jamie. Not every boy on the field had his father at the game, but most of them did. Jamie and Rollin looked like a proud father and son, but they weren't, and that hurt Corra a little.

On the way to their usual hot dog stand after every game, Jamie came up to Corra and hugged her.

"Baby, you were phenomenal today." Corra stroked his back.

"Mom, is my daddy ever coming back?" Jamie asked, with a quiver in his voice.

A lump formed in Corra's throat, big enough to choke a horse. How long would she keep telling her children their father was working in California, and had to stay for a few years? They coped with the divorce pretty well because they were so young. But what was she doing to Jamie?

Corra kneeled down to Jamie and smiled. "Honey, you know your daddy's working in California, but I promise you he'll be home soon."

"Why doesn't he call us?"

The sad look in his eyes tore Corra's heart apart. A few months ago he asked for his daddy, and cried himself to sleep.

She lowered her head. "Baby—"

"Your dad asked me to take care of you until he gets back," Rollin said as he walked up. "Is it okay if Uncle Rollin pitches in for a while?"

Jamie nodded and stepped back from Corra. She stood up with tears so big she could hardly see her baby.

"Hey, Jamie, why don't you go see if your sister wants an ice cream cone. My treat." Rollin pulled a few bills from his pocket and gave them to Jamie.

"Okay, thanks." Wide-eyed, Jamie took off in the direction of his sister and Tayler who were sitting on a bench still eating.

Corra dug into her purse for a tissue and wiped her eyes. Eric's absence was getting harder to cover up.

"Why do you keep telling him that?" Rollin asked.

"Because one day he'll be back."

"Do you want him back?" Rollin looked a little stunned by her answer.

She stopped wiping her eyes. "Hell no, I don't want him back. But right now Jamie needs him in his life. As long as Eric's parents are here he'll eventually come back."

"You truly don't know where he is, do you?" Rollin asked.

"No I don't."

"Well, maybe you should find out for the kids' sake."

She nodded. "I was thinking the same thing when I watched all the fathers and sons gather for pictures. Jamie barely smiled for the picture."

"Why don't you bite the bullet and contact his sister, Cookie? I heard she's a changed woman now that she's found religion. I bet she knows how to reach him. He needs to be a father to his children."

The tears started again and Corra blotted her eyes. She didn't like to let the kids see her cry. Rollin was right. She needed a plan to do something she dreaded, but knew she had to do. Find Eric.

Chapter 6

Chris tackled Monday morning with a vengeance. The usual 9:00 a.m. webinar with his direct reports went off without a hitch. Afterward, he attended a meeting at the Boyle County Chamber of Commerce. He even managed to squeeze in a conference call on his way back to the office. Terry was still conducting interviews for customer support representatives. By the end of next week, the business would be fully staffed, and Chris could relax a little.

He spent the afternoon responding to emails and thinking about Corra. Opposite of his desk was a framed poster that he liked to live by. "Truth builds trust." He hadn't been totally truthful with Corra about why he hadn't contacted her.

It was true, his workload had increased in Philly,

but he knew as well as she did that he could have made an effort to see her. He flew back whenever his parents needed him, and she knew that much about him. But the accident had shaken him and made him second-guess his decisions.

Plus, he'd never been involved with a woman who had children. Corra was the only woman who'd made him want to reconsider his position when it came to children. But, he couldn't exactly tell her that, so instead he'd stayed away.

He leaned back in his seat thinking for a minute. If he truly wanted to start a relationship with her he'd have to overcome his apprehension. And he had to end it now.

He picked up the phone and called Corra on her cell phone.

"Hello."

"Hey, Corra. It's Chris, were you busy?"

"I'm closing shop and going over to the house to talk to Tayler. The Color of Success has an event this week that we need to discuss."

"How long do you think that's going to take? Because I'd like to see you this evening. I thought we could take a ride and talk."

Silence came from her end. Was she trying to decide if she'd give him a chance or not?

"A ride where to?" she finally asked.

"Nowhere in particular. I just want to spend some time with you."

"Really?" Corra asked, sounding surprised.

Chris laughed. "Yes. What time do you think you'll be finished? I can pick you up."

"Don't bother coming out here. I'll call the baby-sitter and you can pick me up at the house. Do you remember where I live?"

He smiled. "I know exactly where you live. How does seven or seven thirty sound?"

"Make it seven thirty."

"Okay, see you then." Chris hung up hoping his plan would bring Corra around. She'd seemed rather cool on the phone just now. He wanted to bring fun-loving, laugh-out-loud Corra back. The rest of Chris's workday was a blur. He ran through everything in anticipation of picking Corra up after work. He didn't even go home to eat; instead, he grabbed some fast food that would no doubt give him heartburn later.

At seven thirty on the nose he pulled up in front of Corra's modest split-level, two-car-garage home. The house had great curb appeal in a family-friendly neighborhood, and conjured up thoughts of a gingerbread house. Several of her neighbors were sitting on their front porches taking in the evening breeze. His hometown had a certain charm that he never found in Philly.

He turned off the engine and jumped out of the car. To his surprise Corra was already walking down the steps. She waved to her neighbors.

He walked over to open the door for her. She looked beautiful in a long sundress with a short jacket. Her toes were painted hot pink in some flat sandals; her purse was slung across her body like the college kids wore theirs.

"As usual, you look great." He leaned in and gave her a quick kiss on the cheek before she could protest.

"Thank you very much, sir." She swiveled into the passenger seat.

"You're welcome, my lady." He waited until she had gathered her dress before he closed the door, then walked around to the driver's side.

"You ready?" he asked, as he started the car.

She shrugged. "I don't know where I'm going, but I trust you won't take me too far. So, I guess I'm ready."

Chris pulled off. He wanted to take Corra to the first place he'd realized he had feelings for her all those years ago. He thought they had an unspoken past that neither of them could have acted on at the time, but he needed confirmation that it wasn't all in his head.

"How are things at the bed-and-breakfast?" he asked.

"Busy," she replied.

"The code to download your new software should arrive this week. Of course, I'll come over to walk you through the setup. I think you'll be very happy with it."

"I hope so."

When Chris drove up to their old high school Corra looked over at him. "We're going to school?"

"We're going to practice." He eased the vehicle to the edge of the parking lot across from the football field and parked. "Come on, let's watch them practice."

After exiting the car, he took hold of Corra's hand as they walked across the grass to the bleachers. Then he helped her climb the steps before taking a seat. Just watching the team brought back memories of being on the field himself and seeing Corra and her friends in the stands watching them.

"When's the last time you played football?" Corra asked.

Chris leaned back on his elbows. "Whew, it's been a while. Maybe five years or more. I used to volunteer with the Boys and Girls Club in Philly so I played around with them a bit. But that's about it. All I do now is watch football."

"I bet you could still play!"

"Oh, I can run the ball, as long as I don't get tackled. One good hit and I'm out of commission."

"Well, I can tell you still work out."

Was that a compliment? Maybe she was coming around. "Almost every day. That's part of my effort to stay in shape. Football or not, I have a business to run."

A play on the field caught their attention and Chris stood and applauded. "Nice move."

"I remember watching you make moves like that. You were good. I had such a crush on you in high school." Corra pressed a palm to her forehead and laughed.

"I'm flattered." Chris was happy the feeling was

mutual. "And I remember looking up in the stands at you and your friends."

"But you were watching Josleen. You had a thing for her."

Chris sat up. "I wasn't looking at Josleen, I was looking at you. A couple of times I wanted to take you to a movie or something after the game."

Corra grew silent again and looked around before responding. "Then why didn't you ask?"

"Come on. You know Rollin would have broken my legs." Chris leaned forward, resting his elbows on his thighs. "I wanted to ask you to my senior prom too, but I valued my life too much for that."

"Rollin wouldn't have hurt you."

"Huh, on the football field Rollin's a different man. One night after a game a bunch of us went to a party and maybe had a little too much to drink. I mentioned something about going out to his house looking for you. He jacked me up against a wall and told me if I ever so much as looked at you wrong he'd make me regret it."

Corra smiled. "He said that?"

"Yeah. He was looking out for you. At that time I was sowing my wild oats, as they call it. So full of myself that I had to have everyone who wanted a piece of me. Rollin didn't want you to get caught up in that."

Corra kept smiling.

"But, then you hooked up with Eric."

"Oh, we're back to him. Whatever happened between you two?"

His dislike for Eric Hayden was not something he wanted to discuss with his ex-wife. "He started dating you."

Practice died down so Chris stood up and held his hand out to Corra. "Come on, I have somewhere else I want to take you."

Never in a million years would she have imagined that he had a crush on her as well. She was a simple country girl. What had he seen in her then? Now she was a single mother of two, yet he still seemed interested in her.

They walked back to Chris's car and he continued to reminisce while he drove around to some of their once popular stomping grounds. Corra continued to laugh and have a good time as he cruised through a park, and by an old ice cream parlor where everybody used to hang out.

"You know, I can't remember when I laughed so hard. How do you remember all of that?" she asked.

"Football didn't take away my sharp memory. I even remember the first time I kissed you out in the back of the barn."

Corra bit her bottom lip. "I wondered if you remembered that. It was the highlight of my freshman year. Even though I believe you actually bumped into me and we accidentally kissed."

"That was no accident," Chris said with a wink.

Corra smiled and looked out the side window.

The date ended because Chris had an early meeting the next morning. He drove Corra home and saw a light on in the living room.

"What time do your kids go to bed?" he asked.

"Mrs. Baker puts them to bed by nine, so they should be fast asleep."

Chris walked her up to the front porch.

"Thank you, Chris. I enjoyed the evening. It was different. A ride down memory lane."

"I hope you don't mind that we didn't go anywhere fancy. I just wanted to spend some time with you."

She smiled. "It was perfect." She dug in her purse for her door keys.

"Uh, I was going to ask if you wanted to—"

The front door swung open, and two little faces peered out.

"Why aren't you in bed?" Corra asked with a hand on her hip.

The door opened farther and a frustrated looking Mrs. Baker shook her head. "I've put them to bed twice now. Every time they hear a car outside they come running down the steps. Quit your gawking, and go on back to bed," she instructed.

They couldn't take their curious little eyes off Chris. Jamie waved and Chris did the same.

Corra opened the screen door and did the introductions. "Katie and Jamie, you remember Mr. Williams, don't you? He helped with the fund-raiser last year."

Jamie's eyes widened with recognition. "Hi, Chris," he said.

"Hey, Jamie, how you doin'?"

Jamie didn't know what to do with his hands as he

suddenly held them over his head, and then around himself. Corra rolled her eyes. Why did he get so shy around Chris?

"Katie, say hello," Corra instructed her.

In typical Katie fashion, she held up her hand and stumbled into her brother's back. Of course, he turned around and pushed her away. Which sent Katie into a whining frenzy.

Corra stepped inside. "Okay, that's it, you two, off to bed right now. Jamie, leave your sister alone." She caught his hand before he grabbed Katie's hair.

"She started it," he exclaimed on his way up the steps.

Corra turned to Chris. "I'll be right back."

Chris smiled, but kept his distance on the front porch.

Corra tucked the kids in while Mrs. Baker cleaned up the living-room-turned-playroom. Corra couldn't help but wonder what Chris thought about her kids.

"I'm sorry." Corra stepped back out onto the porch. "They wanted to see you, and I'm afraid at times Mrs. Baker is no match for them. She's wonderful with them, but they can be stubborn."

Chris turned around with a smile on his face. "Cute kids."

"Yeah, wait until you catch them in the light of day, when they have a full tank of gas. Right now they're operating on fumes, it's bedtime."

"Speaking of which, it's mine as well." He licked his lips and boldly took a step closer to Corra. She immediately held out her hand.

"Good night, Chris."

He smiled and absently scratched behind his ear. "Okay, I need to work for it," he mumbled.

"What was that?" she asked, knowing full well she heard him.

He shook his head. "Nothing. Well, thank you for spending the evening with me. I hope this isn't the last time I see you this week?"

Corra stepped back inside and turned around. "You know where to find me."

Chris backed down the steps. "See you soon."

Chapter 7

Chris walked through the wide central hallway of his fixer-upper and out onto the porch as his father's car pulled into the driveway. Standing between the four columns and two bronze lions that had survived all these years without being vandalized, he felt a real sense of pride. He wanted to lift his head toward town and say, "look at me now," to all the naysayers and haters he'd encountered growing up in Danville.

His father spent many years running errands up to the big house, as it was referred to years ago. But not once had he been invited any farther than the foyer. This was the first time Nathaniel would explore the home he'd admired for so long.

"I see you brought your tools with you," Chris said, pointing to the toolbox in his father's hand.

"Yeah, I figured you'd need more help than me just looking around the place. I might be able to repair something for you."

Chris smiled and patted his father on the back as he stepped up onto the porch. "Thanks, Dad, but I've hired a contractor so we'll let them handle most of the major work."

Nathaniel stood on the porch taking in the lions, the urns that flanked the door, and the balcony above the entrance.

"I remember when they imported those urns. Came all the way from Italy." He slowly started inside the house.

Chris walked in behind him. "They've ripped a lot out, so it looks a little bare right now, but in a few months it'll be beautifully renovated."

"What you plan on doing to the place?"

Chris led the way down the hallway into the center of the house. "I'm going to restore as many original features as I can, but I'm also going to add a few modern touches. I'm adding more closets, updated kitchen appliances, and I'm putting in larger windows. There's not enough natural light for me."

"Most of these old antebellum places don't have large picture windows, but the rooms are plenty big." Nathaniel walked from the library to the living room, then stopped to look at the chandelier hanging between the rooms. "That's an original Schonbek, you know?"

Chris nodded. "I know. It's a thing of beauty."

Nathaniel started down the hall toward the classic staircase, then stopped and turned around to his son. "How many bedrooms in this place?"

"Five. They're all upstairs. Want to see them?"

"In time. Let me ask you something. What do you plan to do with all this house? You don't need all them bedrooms."

Chris laughed. "Maybe not, but I've wanted this place all my life. It's a great investment."

Nathaniel shook his head. "If you say so." Then he scratched his forehead. "Wait until your mother gets a look at this place."

"Come on upstairs. I don't want Mom to see the place until it's finished. Right now it's too dangerous for her to be walking around here, anyway."

Nathaniel followed Chris up the stairs. "At least they have hardwood floors everywhere."

Later, Chris and Nathaniel went to work helping his contractors demo the kitchen. After the contractors left Chris found two chairs and sat them out back by the pool while they had sandwiches.

"What's that building there?" Nathaniel asked, pointing to a structure on the other end of the pool.

"That's the pool house. Fully equipped with a kitchen, bathroom and everything."

Nathaniel smiled and shook his head. "We're going to have some fun pool parties this summer. I can see it already. You're going to have to invite Darlene and her kids down from Louisville."

"Oh, if we get everything finished before the summer is over, it's going to be on and poppin'."

"You can invite your girlfriend and her kids. Kids love to go swimming."

Chris nodded, but didn't say anything.

"You are still seeing her, aren't you?" Nathaniel asked.

"Dad, let me ask you something."

Nathaniel put his sandwich down. "Now I ain't met the girl yet. Don't tell me it's over."

"No. We're getting reacquainted. And the thing is, she has children. A boy and a girl, both in elementary school." He paused and waited for his dad to say what a responsibility that was and that maybe he'd bitten off more than he could chew.

"What's the problem?"

"I'm not sure if I'm ready for that. You know, a ready-made family."

Nathaniel stretched out his long legs and crossed his arms. "You've never been afraid of anything your whole life."

"I didn't say I was afraid."

"Then what do you call it? A single mother's life is tough, and can be challenging for the man who steps into it. But the rewards, ah, the rewards can be great. You went through many obstacles starting your businesses, and look where you are now." Nathaniel spread his arms out toward Chris.

Chris admired his father, but sometimes he just wanted a straight answer. Should he keep seeing the woman or not?

Nathaniel put his arms down. "Chris, you don't need dating advice from me. Follow your heart, and face your fears the same way you have all your life. If it's meant to be, it will be."

His father was right about one thing. Chris was afraid…afraid of the responsibility that came with children. What if he accidentally did something wrong and risked losing Corra over the kids? Was in a situation again like the car accident? He'd agonized over the issue for too long. It was time to quit being afraid.

He stood up. "Well, dinner's over. Ready to find something else to work on?"

Nathaniel stood as well. "Yeah, let's find some woodwork that needs fixing."

Corra sat in the back of the local AME Church listening to Tayler talk to a handful of young girls about the importance of education. The topic of this Wednesday evening's workshop was Education Enhancement. A local college professor was the guest speaker. Every time Tayler gave a presentation, Corra was in awe. With each workshop she learned something new, and gained a measure of confidence in herself.

The Color of Success, a nonprofit organization Tayler and Corra's cousin Nicole started years ago in Chicago, was building momentum in Danville. Since Tayler's relocation they'd held a kickoff meeting, organized a fund-raiser and were officially accepting girls into the program. Unfortunately, her Katie was too young for the program that supported middle school and high school girls.

Most of the girls had been dropped off by a parent. However, a few parents lingered outside the room waiting for their daughters. Corra hadn't recognized any of the girls until the workshop ended. One girl stood out from the rest. She had long braids running down her back, but it was her nose and slanted eyes that identified her as a Hayden. Corra followed her out into the hallway. The child walked right up to Cookie Hayden, Eric's sister. Like her daughter, Cookie had long braids as well. Corra hadn't spoken to Cookie in over three years.

Just then, Cookie glanced up and spotted her. She leaned over and whispered something to her daughter, who ran off with her friends. Cookie crossed her arms and screwed up her face.

Any other time Corra would have ignored Cookie, but she couldn't have planned this better. She needed to find Eric, and like Rollin said, Cookie was her best bet. She swallowed her pride, and reluctantly walked over to her sister-in-law.

"Well, if it isn't Corra Coleman. That is your name, isn't it? You took your name back?" Cookie asked, with a sharp tone.

Corra opened her mouth to respond, but thought better about the smart-alecky response she had in mind. Instead, she cleared her throat and smiled politely, but not genuinely.

"Hi, Cookie. I'm surprised to see you here." Corra had never known Cookie or anyone in her family to attend church.

"Well, you haven't seen me in years, so you'd

probably be surprised about a lot of things." She lowered her arms, and softened the features of her face. "So, you're a part of this organization?" she asked.

Corra nodded. "I am. Rollin's fiancée runs it. I work with her."

Cookie fiddled with her bracelet, examining it as she spoke. "I've heard good things about the organization. And JoJo practically begged me to bring her. I think all of her little friends are involved."

"That's good. It's a great program." Corra held her chin high. This was the first civil conversation they'd had in Corra didn't remember how long.

"Cookie, I'm actually glad I ran into you. I haven't seen Eric in a couple of years and the kids are asking about him. Have you spoken with him lately? Is he still in California?"

Cookie flipped her braids and ran a hand through them. "In all this time you haven't called, or come out to the house asking about him."

Corra caught the neck motion and knew Cookie was about to slip into a bad attitude. Corra maintained her professionalism. "His son would like to see him, Cookie."

"You mean my nephew that I never get to see? The kids you never bring around?" Cookie asked.

Before Cookie lost her composure and embarrassed them both, Corra asked, "Can I speak to you outside a minute?"

"Sure, let's go."

They followed other parents out a side door and walked over to the steps.

"Cookie, I know we haven't been on the best of terms, but I genuinely need to get in contact with Eric. He just disappeared from their lives."

"What you need, some money? Or, are you trying to file for child support when you got sole custody?"

Corra snorted. "No. I'm not asking him for child support. I just want him to get in contact with his kids."

Cookie stared a hole in the ground before she looked up at Corra. "So you really don't know where Eric's been?"

"Somewhere in California was the last I heard. But he hasn't picked up the phone once to call, or write, or do anything for his kids."

"There's a reason he didn't call."

Corra laughed. "There's no reason for a man not to call his kids for two years. I divorced him, not them."

"He was in jail. Eric got into a little financial trouble and spent two years in Los Angeles County Jail paying for it."

Corra's mouth fell open as her fingers spread out against her breastbone. "What did he do?"

Cookie looked around not wanting to be overheard. "He borrowed some money, but they said he stole it. Which he didn't."

Corra wondered if Eric's gambling problem had caught up with him. "Is he still there? Why didn't he tell me?"

"He's out now, but he was too ashamed to tell you."

"So do you have a number for him?"

"No, but the next time he calls I'll tell him you asked about him. I told you because I think you need to know. He wasn't deliberately staying away. And now he's trying to get his life together."

Corra sat down on one of the steps to compose herself. She couldn't imagine Eric in jail. No matter how much she disliked him she would not have wanted to see him go to jail. Thank God the kids didn't have to witness that.

"When you talk to him will you tell him Jamie's playing baseball now and he misses him? And Katie, she's growing up right before my eyes every day."

Cookie sat down on the step below Corra. "I bet they're growing up so fast."

"They are," Corra said in a soft voice. She could feel her throat closing up as sadness consumed her. She wasn't one of those women who tried to keep their ex from his children. She knew the value his presence would have in their lives. Eric had never been a bad father, only a bad husband.

"Uh, why don't you bring the kids around the house some time? We don't have to get along for them to get to know their cousins."

Corra thought about that for a second. Rollin said Cookie had changed, and here she was bringing JoJo to church for a girls' empowerment program.

"I'll think about it," Corra conceded.

Cookie stood up. "Well, if you decide to, here's my cell number." She reached into her purse and produced a business card.

Corra read the card. Econsola Hayden, jewelry consultant. *Maybe she has turned her life around, and hopefully Eric has as well.*

Chapter 8

Corra's horse led the way around the track as she jumped up and down cheering him on. "Come on, number three! Come on, baby!"

Chris had phoned a friend and gotten them access to his corporate suite at Keeneland Racetrack in Lexington. The suite came with your own attendant, table and chairs, and easy access to mutuels to place a bet. A few other people occupied the suite with them.

"Did you see her? That was my filly, she won!" Corra grabbed him by the arm and danced around. Her excitement brought a smile to Chris's face. This is exactly what he wanted, to see her happy.

"How much did you bet on it?" he asked.

"Two dollars," she said with a smile and continued to ooze excitement.

Chris raised a brow. Did anybody over sixteen still bet two dollars on a race? He reached into his pocket and pulled out some money. He handed Corra a fifty-dollar bill. "I lost this race, but whatever you pick for the next one put this on it."

Corra leaned away from him and shook her head. "I can't take your money. Two dollars is good enough. It's all in fun anyway, right? Does it matter if we win or lose?"

"You seem to be doing pretty good so far, so why not increase your bet?"

Corra tiptoed and planted a kiss on Chris's cheek. Her soft lips against his skin caused him to take a deep breath. He looked down into her smiling face and wanted to bend her over backward and devour her in kisses. But, at that moment the attendant walked over to ask if they needed anything. Chris ordered another drink, and then lunch.

In the middle of their meal, Corra leaned over and whispered in Chris's ear.

"Thank you for today. I've never been to a Spring Meet before, nor have I ever sat in a suite. But don't tell anybody."

He held his index finger to his lips. "Mum's the word."

After lunch they returned to betting. Corra was like his good luck charm. Every time he let her choose and place the bet, they won. She came back after picking up an exacta win and handed the money to Chris.

"No, you keep that. You're quite the gambler."

She left the money on the table and shook her head. "I don't want to be a gambler. Serious gambling ruins lives. I'm sticking with my two-dollar bets. I just want to have fun. You keep the money."

Her face took on a more serious tone. Unintentionally, he'd just zapped all the excitement out of her. What had he said?

He pushed the money back to her. "Okay, two dollars a bet it is. We'll have some fun. I didn't mean to upset you."

She nodded. "You didn't. It just brought back some bad memories, that's all."

"Did he have a gambling problem?" Chris asked. He knew Eric had some problems, but he'd never known to what extent.

Corra snorted. "That's putting it mildly."

Chris could have shot himself in the foot for taking her to the track when her ex had a gambling problem. "I'm sorry I brought you here. I didn't know."

"Oh, no. Don't be sorry. I like it here. I don't have a problem, do you?"

Her wide-eyed facial expression said it all. She wanted to make sure she wasn't getting involved with another gambler.

He put his arm around her shoulder for reassurance. "The only serious gambling I do is in business. And even then I don't make a move unless the odds are in my favor."

She took a deep breath and her shoulders relaxed.

"However, I'm willing to bet that nothing short of miraculous is about to happen between us. Something that should have happened a long time ago. You were meant to be mine." He leaned down and kissed her gently on the forehead.

The Greek Alumni crowd had checked out on Friday and Saturday. Sunday's group was a little more reserved, which left the house nice and quiet.

After church, followed by Jamie's baseball game, Corra and the kids were wiped out. But that didn't stop her from getting them dressed and out to the house for dinner.

This Sunday evening's dinner at the Coleman House was extra special. Tracee had prepared a new dessert which they always sampled on the staff before serving to guests. Rita's husband, Wallace, owned an auto body shop that was closed on Sunday, so he often joined them around the large kitchen table for dinner.

Tracee pulled her apple-gingerbread cobbler from the oven. "If you like it, we're adding it to the menu." She scooped generous portions into each bowl.

That's what Corra had been smelling all through dinner.

"Now that's what I'm talkin' about," Rollin said as he dug in.

"Tracee, this cobbler is delicious. I vote we add this to the menu," Corra said, casting the first vote.

"Oh, I definitely agree with Corra," Tayler added.

"Me too," Rollin added.

"I fourth that," Kyla added.

Everyone turned to Wallace who was still eating. He stopped once he realized all eyes were on him. "Hell yeah, add my vote."

Tracee clapped. "It's unanimous then." She turned to a beaming Rita. "We have a new menu item."

After dinner, Corra rounded up Jamie and Katie who were stretched out in Rollin's bedroom watching a movie. She poked her head in. "Okay you two, time to go."

They slowly began to move with their eyes still glued to the television. Rollin walked up behind her.

"I heard about your day at the races. I'm glad to see you and Chris are hitting it off."

"Yeah, and he told me about all the years you wouldn't let him ask me out."

"In high school Chris was your typical jock, and you were one of the good girls. Trust me, I did you a favor. No doubt he's a good man, but back then I wasn't going to let him mess around with my little sister." Rollin pulled the door to his bedroom closed.

"I bet you saved yourself for your husband, didn't you?"

Corra's mouth fell open. "That is none of your business." Although he'd been right. "You don't know what I was doing, or who I was doing it with, thank you."

"Hey, all I'm saying is I know how you were

raised. That's why I said you weren't ready for Chris."

She tilted her head. "Regardless, I bet I'm ready now."

Chapter 9

"Girl, if these kids don't stay in bed I'm going to have to get out my belt." Corra held the phone down. "Jamie, where you goin'?"

"To get some water," he said from the hallway.

"You've had enough water. Get back in bed. I don't know why y'all want to test me tonight. If I hear you come out of that room one more time I'm coming in there…"

Jamie poked his head into her bedroom. "My throat's dry."

Corra sat on her bed with her feet up unwinding from a busy Sunday while detailing her day at the races to Sharon.

"Okay, go get you some water and bring it up with you."

"Is he okay?" Sharon asked through the phone.

"Yeah, he's fine." Corra frowned as soon as Jamie left the room. He looked fine, but he also breathed as if he'd run up the stairs already.

"So finish telling me about your date," Sharon said.

After Corra shared some exciting details about the race day Sharon coaxed her for more. "What else can I say, it was great. Chris knows some people in high places. I've only looked up at those boxes. I never imagined I'd be sitting up there one day."

"Chris is a good guy, Corra. I like him."

"Yeah, he is. I've always liked Chris. But, sometimes I think why me, when he can have any woman he wants? And I can't imagine the women he had in Philadelphia. I'm surprised he's still single."

"Maybe he's been waiting for you?"

"Girl, please. That man has not been waiting for me. After the accident I didn't think I'd see him again. Not in a dating capacity anyway. It was as if his whole presence at the fund-raiser was a dream. He came along and helped us, then poof, he was gone."

"Like Cinderella in reverse, huh?"

"Yeah, just like that."

"But the prince has come back to get his princess. Just like in Cinderella."

"Sharon, stop fantasizing everything."

"I can't help it. I believe in happily-ever-afters. Maybe in school you wouldn't have been perfect for each other. But now that you've both grown and matured, the time is right."

Corra laughed. "I don't know about all that. I'm just going to hold on and enjoy the ride."

"That's it, girl. And haven't you been celibate for a long time now?"

Corra sat up and swung her legs off the side of the bed. "Okay, I'm not talking about my sex life tonight. I'm going to hang up now and go check on my son. I'll talk to you tomorrow."

"Aw, you're no fun."

Corra hung up and went to check on Jamie. The house was quiet as she walked down the hall and eased the door open to his room. He had the covers pulled up over his shoulders and was fast asleep. She tiptoed over to the other side of the bed and watched him sleep for a few seconds. His breathing was normal with a light snore. She tiptoed back out of the room and returned to her bedroom.

After her nightly beauty ritual, she lay back to read a book. The phone rang. Before she snatched the phone from its cradle, she wondered who was calling this late. She glanced at the caller ID, but didn't recognize the name or number.

"Hello."

"Hey, Corra. I heard you were looking for me?"

Corra dropped her book. "Eric?"

After a long pregnant pause he cleared his throat. "Yeah, it's me."

Corra sat up. She hadn't heard his voice in over two years. She didn't know whether to curse him out or thank him for calling. Seems like her chat with Cookie worked.

"How are the kids?" he asked.

"They're fine." Still unsure how she wanted to handle this call, she walked over and closed the door to her bedroom. "Why haven't you called them?"

"It's a long story—"

"Yeah, I bet it is. I know where you've been."

"Who told you?"

"Cookie."

"Yeah well, I didn't want to call from jail so—"

"Eric, what happened? How did you wind up in jail?"

"I kind of got caught up in something and made a stupid mistake. But I've put that all behind me now. I don't gamble anymore, Corra. I'm sorry I screwed everything up between us, but I didn't mean to walk out of my kids' lives."

Oh, yeah. It's just me you meant to walk out on. And what about the cheating? Are you still a cheater? Or just a liar? "You need to see your kids, Eric. Or call them if you can't make it down here."

"I'm in Danville now."

"How long have you been here?"

Silence from the other end. Then she heard what sounded like him putting his hand over the phone.

"Look, Corra, I gotta go. This isn't my phone. I do want to see the kids, so how about I come by tomorrow? What time do they get home from school?"

Tomorrow! Corra wasn't prepared mentally to see Eric so soon.

"Jamie has baseball practice after school. He won't be home until around five."

"Okay, how about I stop by at six."

"We'll probably be eating dinner around that time."

"Then how about seven?"

God knows she did not want to see Eric. But, she asked for this because she didn't want to be one of those mothers who kept their kids from their fathers. "Yeah, seven o'clock is good."

"Okay, I'll see you then."

Corra hung the phone up and just sat there staring into the floor. Eric had avoided her question about how long he'd been in town. If he'd been that eager to see his kids he would have come around as soon as he returned. But, Cookie must have confirmed that she didn't want child support from him. Bastard.

Thankfully, Corra hadn't mentioned her phone call from Eric to Jamie or Katie. Monday evening came and went—no Eric. On Tuesday when he called to apologize and rescheduled for the next day, she blew a gasket.

"How come I knew you were going to do this? You are still so predictable and unreliable."

"Corra, hold on. It's not my fault."

"It never is, Eric." Livid with herself for thinking for one moment that he might do the right thing, she began to have regrets.

"I promise I'll be there tomorrow evening, I'm sorry."

She lowered her forehead into her palm and kept telling herself, *it's for the kids.* "Okay, but don't stand them up again." She hung the phone up questioning herself as to whether she'd done the right thing or not.

Less than a minute later, the phone rang again.

"Hello," she answered in a cheerful voice when she saw Chris's name on caller ID.

"Hey, what are you doing this evening?"

A flash of excitement crept into her. "Well, I was about to see if the kids have any homework. Why? Did you have something in mind?"

"Yeah, I've been working on something that I really want you to see. And this evening would be perfect."

"Hum, this is kind of short notice," she said, with a little hesitation in her voice.

"I know. I'm sorry. I just got a little excited."

"Well, let me call Mrs. Baker to see if she can babysit for a while. I'll call you right back."

"Great."

She hadn't seen or spoken to Chris since Saturday, so she wondered what he was so excited about. After they hung up she quickly called Mrs. Baker who happily agreed to watch the kids for her. The only caveat was she had to bring them to her house.

Corra called Chris back and arranged to meet him after she dropped off the kids. Curiosity plagued her as she rode through town headed for their rendezvous spot. The minute she pulled into the parking lot she spotted Chris's Cadillac. She parked next to him, got out of her car and into his.

"Thanks for coming on such short notice. You look nice." He started the car.

Corra tried not to blush. She'd put on one of her favorite sundresses since it was almost eighty degrees out.

"Thank you. I feel like a woman cheating on her husband, meeting in a parking lot like we're having an affair."

Chris laughed. "I'm sorry, I didn't mean to make you feel like a scandalous woman. I had some business to take care of in the area and didn't want to lose too much sunlight."

"Hum, now I'm really wondering where you're taking me."

"Trust me, you'll be surprised. It's someplace important to me so I wanted you to see it."

"Okay." Corra noted the serious tone to Chris's voice. She couldn't wait to see whatever he had to show her.

He pulled out of the parking lot. "I promise I won't keep you out too late. How was your day today?"

"Busy. I swear I work more at the bed-and-breakfast than I ever did at Save-A-Lot. Some days I feel like a jack-in-the-box. Jumping from one role to another."

"Is the software helping out any?"

"Oh yes! I've loaded inventory and created helpful reports. So far, I like it. Tayler loves it. And Rollin's even a fan, but he said he would talk to you about it. So, he might have a few questions."

"Well, I'm glad to hear it's working out for you guys. I knew it would. Once you get everything implemented it should cut your workload in half."

"So, did you create the program? I know you're a computer whiz and all."

Chris laughed. "Me a whiz. Now that's funny. 3C has a team of developers working on new programs all the time. We have a suite of applications just for the hospitality industry. I have some input, but the design isn't all mine by any means."

"I've been meaning to ask you, what does 3C stand for?"

"The three owners of the business, Chris, Cameron and Carl. And Evolution because we plan to continue growing, evolving. We've found our niche, but there's plenty of room for growth in the industry."

Corra stared at Chris admiringly. He'd always been a smart guy in high school, but she never knew he had such an entrepreneurial spirit. "And this is your second company?"

"Yep. The first one was built to sell. I knew if I made it attractive enough I could make a profit once it sold."

Corra was more focused on Chris's businesses than where they were going. So, when he turned off the highway down a road that led to the old Whitfield home, she didn't know what to think. No one had lived in that house for years.

"You're a smart businessman. But I have a question for you? What the hell are we doing here?"

"You'll see," Chris said, as he pulled up close to the front entrance.

From the looks of all the building material alongside the house, it was being worked on. At one time it belonged to the richest family in Danville. Who owned it now?

"Come on, this is what I wanted to show you." Chris climbed out of the car and Corra did the same. He walked around to close her door.

He took her hand and they walked up to the front porch. When he reached in his pocket and pulled out a key to open the door, Corra's eyes widened.

He pushed the door open and looked back at her, she was stunned.

"After you," he said.

Confused, she walked in, her eyes darting around the foyer and beyond to the bare drywall and dusty floors, settling on the magnificent chandelier above. "Chris, whose house is this?"

"Moi!" he said, pointing to himself before he closed the door and walked in behind her. "I'm restoring most of the rooms. Come on, let me give you the grand tour."

Corra wanted to stop him and ask, "No, really, whose house is this?" He did not just tell her he'd purchased the oldest, grandest home in all of Danville. Chris took her hand and walked her through the house pointing out his plans for each room. She was too stunned to speak.

In the master bedroom he held the balcony doors open as she stepped out to enjoy the view. The trees blowing in the wind and the chirping sound of the birds was so calming and serene. She could imagine herself standing there with her morning cup of coffee, dressed in her robe.

"Nice view, huh?" Chris asked, as he walked up behind her.

"The best. What a way to start your morning. And it's big enough for a small table and two chairs."

He stood behind her and reached around placing his hands on the railing. "So you gonna sit out here and have breakfast with me?" he asked.

Corra wanted to lean back against his big hard body and have him wrap his arms around her. Secretively, she'd thought about Chris holding her that way for years. She could feel his breath against her neck, he was so close. She bit her lower lip and shrugged. "I don't know. Maybe one day."

Chris backed away from her and took her hand again. "Then I'd better speed up renovations."

Chapter 10

They continued the tour until Chris walked Corra out the back door. "I'm going to put a ramp in back here so my mother doesn't have to take the steps if she doesn't want to."

"Chris, can I ask you about your mother's health? I never knew what was wrong with her."

"She has a debilitating case of fibromyalgia. It was diagnosed when I was in junior high. She's always in pain."

"Oh, wow! I know I used to see your father in Save-A-Lot all the time. I've only seen your mother with him a few times. Does she work?" Corra followed Chris to a set of chairs on the back patio that looked over the property.

He shook his head. "She used to be an elementary school teacher, but she's been disabled most of my life."

"I'm sorry, I didn't know that."

"Thanks. It's not something I talk about a lot. She suffered for a long time before the diagnosis. When I was younger I used to get upset because she missed a lot of school activities. By the time I started playing football, I understood she couldn't make the games."

"She never saw you play?"

"She saw a few games. But, the pain kept her away most days. And my dad, being the good husband he was, stayed at home taking care of her most of the time."

"That must have been hard on you."

He shrugged. "You get over it. They attended the most important games. She came to the All-Star game, and that was good enough for me."

"Are you keeping the pool?" Corra asked, to change the subject. She wanted to know about his mom, but she didn't want to cause him to relive any painful memories. She remembered Chris being an outsider, and now she had an idea.

"Of course. Would you come over and swim?"

"Can I bring the kids?" she asked, hoping he wouldn't have a problem with that.

"You most certainly can. A pool party might be the first thing I do once I move in. You guys are welcome anytime."

"Chris, you're really moving in here by yourself?"

"Of course I am. I've wanted this house ever since I saw it for the first time from the school bus."

"Wow, you're gonna rock this town. A young successful black man living in an antebellum mansion that likely belonged to slave owners."

Chris laughed. "I don't think the house is that old. What I plan to do is change the perception of how a young black man can live."

The sun was setting now and Corra knew their time was winding down, but there was so much more to see. "What's that building over there?" she asked, pointing at what looked like another house beyond the pool.

Chris stood up and reached for her hand. "That's the pool house. Come on, let me show you."

Corra took his hand and they walked along the side of the huge empty pool with a frog on each end. "What are the frogs for?"

"They're fountains. They run on a pump. Once the pool is filled, water runs up and spouts out through their mouths. I don't know if they work or not, but that's what they're meant to do."

"Fancy."

"I love all the trees back here. Complete privacy. And at night, it's pitch black. I'm thinking of installing some solar lights."

Chris opened the door to the pool house and Corra was completely blown away by its size. This was a complete house that smelled a little musty, but that was it. She stepped into the living area, and could see the kitchen. "Wow, Chris, this is much larger than I expected it to be."

He gave her a tour of the two bedrooms, full bath and kitchen.

"Okay, there's nothing antebellum about this pool house."

"Yeah, I figure the owners added it after they purchased the house. My dad said they had a couple of sons, so possibly one of the sons lived out here and wanted something a little more modern."

"Is there a laundry room?" she asked.

"Down here." He walked in the opposite direction back through the living room and beyond the kitchen. He opened a closet door. "Looks like a stacked washer and dryer were in here. Not a laundry room, more like a closet."

"Yeah, but that's nice. This was a great little bachelor's pad for one of those lucky guys."

"It sure was. And far enough from the main house to feel like you weren't living at home. I bet they had some wild parties out here."

"And imagine the girls they brought out here."

"Oh yeah, I know if I had a pad like this while living at home I would have—"

Corra placed her hands on her hips and twisted her lips up at Chris. He stopped talking. "You would have what? Had a revolving door installed. Different girl every weekend."

Chris threw his palms up. "I didn't say that. I was about to say I would have snuck you over. Forget what Rollin or your father said. You would have been all mine."

His left brow twitched as he smiled at her. Corra

wagged her finger at him. "Nice save. I know that wasn't what you were about to say, but I like that."

Chris dropped the smile and moved closer to her. "I would have. We would have been out here making love all night long."

"Chris, we were kids."

He lowered his gaze at her. "Kids don't make love? Or what they think at the time is love?"

For a split second, Corra thought back to how young she was having sex with Eric. "I suppose you're right."

He moved even closer, reaching for her hands and intertwining their fingers. "Would you have come out here with me?"

She watched him study her, with curiosity in his eyes. He wanted to know how she felt about him. She nodded and lowered her voice. "Nothing would have stopped me."

Chris let go of her fingers and wrapped his arm around her waist, pressing her against him. He lowered his head and she closed her eyes. When his lips touched hers, her knees weakened. He gave her a soft kiss on the lips at first, then he opened his mouth and changed her world forever.

The moment Corra had fantasized about for so long, but thought would never happen, had arrived. She'd secretively been in love with Chris long before she ever met Eric.

Corra welcomed Chris's embrace and kissed him as if she were trying to make up for all the years they were not together, but should have been. She lost all inhibitions and tried to rip his clothes from his body. His hands were all over her back, her waist, her neck, any and everywhere he could get them.

Chris couldn't get enough of the sweet taste of Corra's lips. His body was on fire and his mind was racing with a way to make love to her right now. He wanted her naked and in his bed. She tugged at his clothes and ran her hands under his shirt. He ached for her so bad at the moment all that mattered was being inside her. She moaned into his mouth, and casting good judgment aside he backed her up until she touched the wall.

She was a smart, hardworking woman who undoubtedly had no idea the effect she had on him. She had a body that would make any men stop in their tracks after only one glance.

He pulled his head back to catch his breath, and slid the straps from her dress off her shoulders. He kissed her there. She smelled like fresh-cut flowers. She had no idea how special she was to him.

She reached up and stopped him from undoing the top button of her dress.

His brows furrowed. "What's wrong?"

"Chris, are we really doing this? You know I'm a package deal. Whoever dates me has to essentially date my kids too. They're the most important thing in my life and I won't let any man come before them."

He nodded. "I'm not asking you to. I've been thinking about this ever since the fund-raiser. Ever since I learned Eric was out of your life. I'll admit

I had to think about it for a minute, but this is what I want."

"Is that the real reason I didn't hear from you after you went back to Philly? You had to think about us?"

"Maybe a little. But, I was busy like I said, and to tell the truth, I had to come to terms with our car accident. I wouldn't lie to you. Ever." He got lost in the deep, dark brown pools of her eyes. He had to assure this woman that he was ready for her package and wouldn't shy away.

He yearned to feel her skin against his. His fingers ached from the need to touch her. For her to touch him. But not out here, not like this. He took a deep breath, kissed her shoulder again before fixing her dress. "Come on, let's go back up to the house."

Back in the main house Chris asked Corra, "So, how do you like the house?"

"Yes, it's amazing. I still can't believe you bought it. Who's working on it?"

"I am." He walked around turning off lights.

"No, I mean who's doing all the physical renovation work?"

"I've hired a general contractor for the major work, but I'm doing a lot of the restoration work myself, with my dad's help."

Corra stopped. "You know how to restore a house?"

He chuckled. "Yes, I do. Remember I used to work construction every summer. And my dad taught me everything I need to know about woodworking."

On the way out Corra stopped and rubbed her

hand across one of the lions positioned at the entrance. "You're keeping these aren't you?"

"You like them?"

She looked up at him. "I do. They remind me of you, actually. Muscular, with a powerful build, impressive, quiet."

Chris grabbed her hand. "Okay, let's stop while you're ahead. I've got a roar like a lion too. And as much as I want you to hear it tonight, I don't think you'll get to. So let's get you home."

Chris clenched his jaws and willed himself to keep going until Corra was inside the car. Trying to have sex with her inside his dusty renovation was not how he wanted their first time to be. They had plenty of time to be together. And one thing he did have in common with a lion, was patience.

Chapter 11

Because it was dark Chris insisted on following Corra to Mrs. Baker's to pick up the kids. Then he followed her home. Jamie and Katie begged to see inside Chris's car, and proceeded to touch and inquire about every button. Corra was thankful Chris didn't mind, and seemed to enjoy explaining all the features.

After she ushered the kids to bed she walked back down to the front door where Chris waited.

"Thank you for seeing me home safely."

"Not a problem. I don't think I could take it if something happened to you again while you were in my company."

Corra started to make a joke about the car accident, but the serious look on Chris's face caused her to change her mind. The accident hadn't been a laughing matter. Someone could have been killed. "You know that car came out of nowhere. There wasn't anything you could do. I've told you that before."

He lowered his head. "Yeah, I know. But I still go back to that night and think if I had done something different—"

"Stop thinking about it. What's done is done. I'm fine now. The experience caused Rollin to keep the bed-and-breakfast open, and I'm happy working there. All's well that ends well."

Chris glanced up the steps before pulling Corra into his arms. She wrapped her arms around his neck and met his kiss with all the longing she'd harbored for him all day.

He released her and whispered, "Thank you. My dad told me the same thing, but I think I needed to hear it from you."

Corra realized he'd been walking around feeling guilty about his involvement in an accident he never caused.

"I'll see you tomorrow?" he asked.

"Sure, after work. Wait! No. Uh, I have something to do after work tomorrow. How about Thursday?"

Chris nodded. "Okay, we'll include the kids next time."

Corra bit her bottom lip to keep from gushing all over the place. Just what she wanted, a man who not only thought of her, but thought of her kids.

"That sounds great."

He opened the front door. "Okay, don't work too hard tomorrow. I'll be in touch."

Corra said goodbye, and then stood in the door until Chris pulled off. She could have told him Eric was coming by to see his kids, but why ruin a perfectly good night. It was apparent from his comment earlier that Chris still didn't care for Eric. Besides, the visit had nothing to do with Chris.

Half past seven and Eric still hadn't shown up. The kids had finished their homework and were about to take their baths. Corra had hoped Eric would show up before that time, but she wasn't waiting for him.

After their baths she walked down to the front door to peek out the window one more time hoping Eric would be pulling up. When she pulled the curtain back a figure moved into view. She jumped back, thrown off for a second. Then she looked again. It was Eric pacing across the front porch.

Corra cautiously opened the front door. Eric turned around, took a deep breath, and then smiled. Once a handsome man, he now looked thinner and older than his thirty-two years.

"Hey, Corra. I was about to ring the bell."

He cleared his throat and shoved his hands deep down into his pockets.

"Come on in." She held the door open.

Eric walked past her and she was shocked at the dramatic decline in his appearance. He'd always been very particular about his clothes and shoes. But, he looked as if he'd slept in his clothes and his shoes had seen better days.

He turned around and clasped his hands together. "Thanks again for letting me visit the kids. I know I owe you an explanation, but can I see the kids first?"

"Sure. I didn't tell them you were coming."

"Why not?" he asked, as he followed her.

"And have you not show up! Do you know what that does to a child?"

"I'm so sorry for everything." He looked up with tears in his eyes.

Corra didn't give a shit about his tears. "I'll go tell them you're here. Have a seat."

"Corra."

She stopped when he called her, and turned around.

Eric tried to give her his sexy smile that used to make her giggle. "You look nice."

His smile had no effect on her whatsoever. "Thank you." She turned around and kept walking.

Upstairs Corra pulled Jamie and Katie into her room and explained that their father was back, and downstairs. Jamie almost tore the bedroom door off the hinges, he was so eager to get downstairs. Katie, however, was a little more reserved.

"Mommy, is Daddy back from work for good?"

Corra kissed her cheek. "I don't know, honey, you'll have to ask him. Aren't you excited to see your daddy?"

Katie nodded. "Are you coming too?"

"I'm right behind you, sugar."

As Corra followed Katie down the steps she could hear Eric and Jamie getting reacquainted. Jamie was in tears he was so happy. Corra found a spot on the couch and watched a hesitant Katie go to her daddy, who smothered her in kisses and hugs. Corra's heart overflowed with joy for her kids. They held no grudges against their father who'd, unbeknownst to them, abandoned them for two years. Corra, on the other hand, was a different story.

Eric spent time with his kids, while Corra cleaned up the kitchen and did any other housework she could find to keep her busy. She wanted to give him time to get caught up on every ball game, play and field trip they proceeded to tell him about.

Bedtime came two hours later, to Jamie and Katie's dismay. Eric promised to come back the next day, so they agreed to go to bed. Corra hoped he wasn't lying to them.

Eric found her in the kitchen cleaning out the microwave.

"Well, they're all tucked in. They said you already made them take a bath. Jamie was pretty adamant about that." Eric pulled out a kitchen chair and sat down.

Corra looked at him and thought, *did I ask you to have a seat?* "Thank you for putting them to bed, and spending some time with them tonight." She didn't move from the microwave, nor put down the sponge. Maybe he would leave if she looked busy.

"Don't thank me. You make me feel like a heel."

She shrugged. "Well, if the shoe fits."

"Corra, I know you're mad at me, and you have every right to be mad. I had a problem. I was addicted. It took me a long time to admit that, but I can be a man about it now. I let gambling come between me and my family. It destroyed every good relationship I had."

"You mean none of your ladies stood by your side while you spent two years working out your gambling problems."

Eric lowered his gaze, and Corra had to restrain herself to keep from grabbing something to hit him over the head with.

"I'm sorry about that too. I never meant to hurt you. I just got caught up in my own bullshit. I was out of control."

She walked over to the sink, wrung out her sponge, and placed it in the drying rack. *Bullshit! I don't want to hear all these lies!*

"I went out to California to make some money. I wanted to pay you back for every dime I spent of ours. But I didn't have my head on straight and wound up…well, you know. The two years I was away allowed me to think straight and get some help. Believe it or not, it was the best thing for me."

Corra dried her hands and examined Eric for the first time since he'd arrived. She'd always been able to tell when he was lying. Like when he tried to convince her he went fishing with his buddies one weekend and she saw those particular guys downtown the same night. The next day he couldn't look her in the eye when she asked about the trip. Tonight, he held her gaze. In fact, it looked as if his eyes were begging her to believe him.

"Did jail cure you from cheating as well?"

"No, maturity has. I was a young jerk who didn't realize how good he had it. I'd never really had anything before so I didn't know how to handle it. But, I do now."

She cleared her throat and walked over to get a glass of water. She didn't want to sit down with him. He'd already overextended his stay.

Eric leaned forward in his chair resting his elbows on his knees. "Corra, I know this might be too much to ask right now, but I need you to forgive me for my past transgressions. I'm a changed man, really I am. I cried many a night thinking about what I did to you…to our family. I lay in bed and closed my eyes hoping to see Jamie and Katie again. I missed them so much."

She almost choked on her water. "Is that why you didn't contact them once you returned?"

That left leg of his started shaking, as it did whenever he was nervous about something.

"I didn't want to see them like this. I lost everything. I flew back from California with only a change of clothes to my name. But I'm waiting to hear about a job now. Once I get it, I hope you'll let me spend more time with you and the kids?"

Oh, hell! Eric had returned and Corra had just started dating his nemesis, Chris.

"Eric, the kids would love nothing more than to spend more time with you. Me, however, I've moved on, we don't need to spend time together." The last thing she wanted was Eric back in her life.

He nodded. "I understand. I knew I couldn't just walk back into your life as if nothing happened. But I can prove myself to you." He stood up.

Corra took a few steps back. "The only people you need to worry about proving something to, are your kids. Be the father they need. You can never be the man I need again."

He held both hands over his heart. "Oh, I'd forgotten about how brutally honest you can be. Still a straight shooter huh, Corra?"

"It's the only way I know how to be."

He turned around and slowly walked out of the kitchen. She followed him to the front door, thankful the evening was over.

"Well, now that I'm back maybe we can work out a schedule or something so I can take the kids sometimes."

When he turned around Corra was shaking her head with her arms crossed. "I have sole custody. Those kids will not be leaving here with you. You're welcome to come by and visit as long as I'm here."

He opened the front door. "Okay, if that's how we're gonna play it."

"That's how it is."

"Yeah, I was just hoping you'd see it in your heart to bend a little since I haven't seen them in so long."

She shook her head. "Court order."

"Okay, well we wouldn't want to go against a

court order, would we? I guess I'll see them the next time I see you," he said with a smile.

Corra nodded. She didn't like the crafty smile on Eric's face. The old Eric would have exploded by now and gotten mad at her. This Eric stood on the porch smiling like everything was right with the world. Or, was he up to something that would make her regret looking him up?

Chapter 12

Friday morning went a little smoother for Corra as far as getting the kids off to school. When the bus driver turned the corner, Jamie and Katie were still in the house, but headed out. The bus driver never even honked his horn. Corra was only a few minutes behind them headed for work.

The ladies of the house were having an 8:00 a.m. meeting to discuss the upcoming nuptials between Tayler and Rollin, and new product lines for the B&B. When Corra arrived everyone was eating breakfast.

"Morning, ladies," Corra greeted her family.

Tayler looked bright and cheerful in a simple yellow sundress and sandals. The color complemented her complexion, and her cute short hairstyle made her look youthful. "Good morning, Corra."

"Hey, Corra." Kyla had on her usual khaki pants and a beige polo shirt, which gave her thin frame an even longer look. For weeks Kyla had tried to talk Rollin into some resemblance of a uniform for the staff, but he hadn't agreed on anything yet.

"What's up? Girl, grab yourself a plate." Tracee, Kyla's older sister and one of Corra's favorite cousins, still had on her apron that protected her white slacks and top from any spills. A hairnet covered her natural hair, which was styled big this morning.

Corra grabbed a plate and joined them at the kitchen table.

"How'd it go getting the kids off this morning?" Kyla asked.

Corra smiled. "Better, believe it or not. I tell you, we're getting this thing down to a science." Every morning Corra entertained with a new story detailing their attempts to meet the school bus.

"But isn't school out in a couple of weeks?" Kyla asked.

"Yes, school's almost out, but kids are a work in progress. You'll understand someday."

"Well, Corra, we're glad you made it early." Tayler interjected. "Ladies, can we talk while we eat?"

"Sure." Everyone agreed.

Tayler kicked off the meeting going down her checklist. Kyla confirmed there would be a variety of flowers for the wedding. And Tracee confirmed she and Rita had the food and cake covered.

"Okay, I've capped the guest list at fifty. Reverend Daniels is scheduled to perform the ceremony, and Rollin's booking the music."

"Oh, no! Don't tell me you're leaving anything up to him?" Corra said, afraid of the outcome.

Tayler laughed. "He's assured me he can handle that."

"Girl, he can't even settle on a best man," Tracee added. "You know I love my cousin, but he takes too long to make up his mind. You'd better find a band yourself."

Kyla spoke up. "I can help with that. There's this really cool top-forty band at school that also does weddings. They perform around town all the time, so maybe we can get together and go see them."

Corra shook her head from side to side, and Tracee snickered.

"What? Why are you laughing?" Kyla asked Tracee.

"Because she knew you were going to suggest a country band," Corra said.

Kyla shrugged. "But, I'm telling you they're good. The Jackson Brothers. They performed at the dean's annual fund-raiser last year."

"That's the dean of agriculture, right?" Corra asked.

Kyla crossed her arms. "Okay, just forget about it. I guess you'd rather have some rap or old school band."

"Nooo." Everyone cried out in unison.

Tayler cleared her throat. "Kyla, thank you for the suggestion. It wouldn't hurt to catch one of their shows before we count them out. Let me know when and where they're playing, and I'll get Rollin to attend with me."

Kyla's chin rose. "Thank you, Tayler. I'm sure you'll be pleasantly surprised."

Corra and Tracee gave each other skeptical looks.

"Ladies, for the remainder of the meeting let's discuss our outstanding projects. The other day Tracee mentioned expanding our food line with cakes and pies. I love that idea, and I know we can make that happen."

"And don't forget my educational program," Kyla added. "Once my proposal is accepted, the Boyle County school system will become another customer for the farm."

"Great, Kyla," Tayler responded.

"And I've been keeping notes of all our wedding research. I think we have the beginnings of a bed-and-breakfast wedding package. Small, intimate weddings that book the whole house up. Other B&Bs in town offer wedding packages. But, they don't have an on-site baker or caterer like we have. We can become a destination wedding venue, of sorts."

Tayler laughed. "I love it. New products, new packages, I swear, we're going to outgrow ourselves if we're not careful."

To Corra, all of these ideas sounded like things her mother would have loved to do herself. While everyone kept throwing out suggestions, she imagined her mother getting the house ready for a wedding.

Dressing the house up for the occasion and having it displayed in the local paper.

Today's meeting ended the way they always did, on the subject of men. Tracee stood up and gathered the empty plates from the table.

"Corra, you must be over there thinking about Chris," Tracee pointed out.

"He's the furthest thing from my mind right now."

"Oh, Corra. Drop the act," Tayler said. "We know how much you like Chris, and it's obvious the feeling's mutual."

"Shoot, Corra, consider yourself lucky. Chris is a catch. I've been back for almost six months and haven't had one date yet," Tracee added, as she filled the dishwasher.

"Tracee, you need to stop being so particular, and see past a man's exterior," Kyla said.

"Chile, please." Tracee rolled her eyes. "How are you going to give me advice when you're married to your studies. I can't even remember the last time I saw you with a man."

Kyla glanced at Corra before clearing her throat. "You're right, the University of Kentucky and my studies are my man. And right now I have a date with my research project." She stood up. "My boss is probably looking for me now. If we're finished I'll get back to work."

"Girl, give it a break. Rollin's not looking for you. You're just trying to get out of here unscathed." Tracee laughed, as Kyla hurried around the table toward the back door.

"My personal business will remain just that—personal. If you need me I'll be out taking soil samples." She opened the door and rushed out.

Corra chuckled, "Kyla is such an introvert. If she was dating somebody she'd probably never tell us. But after the way she ran out of here, you never know."

Tracee closed the dishwasher and turned it on. "So Tayler found Rollin, and Corra, you have Chris. Now baby sister might have somebody. I'm not doing something right."

Tayler closed her laptop and stood from the table. "You're not doing anything wrong. Just be yourself. There's somebody out there for everybody."

A few minutes later, Corra found Tayler at the front desk alone. She had something she wanted to talk to her about. She valued her opinion when it came to men. Tayler had far more experience with wealthy men than she had.

Tayler looked up. "Is something on your mind?"

Corra took a deep breath. "Actually, it is. I was supposed to see Chris yesterday, but he was busy. Instead, he called and invited me to the Kentucky Oaks."

Wide-eyed, Tayler stopped typing. "What are you doing here? It's today!"

"I'm not going." Corra let out a deep sigh and leaned against the counter. "I told him I didn't like crowds."

"Corra, why did you say that?" Tayler asked, looking baffled.

Corra shrugged. "I don't know. One minute things were moving too slow, then things started moving too fast. He's not that same cocky kid I used to dream about. He's this grown-ass man, with a lot of money, who wants to take me places and I'm just not used to that."

Tayler sat back on her stool. "I remember a conversation we had last year about you finding a man that would love you and your children. Chris is that guy. So get used to it. You two belong together. I can see that, why can't you?"

Corra shrugged. She could see it, but for some reason she was scared. Maybe it was because Eric was back. Eric hated Chris. But then she didn't want Eric, so why was she scared?

Tayler crossed her arms. "Okay, Tracee's looking for a good man. Want me to hook them up?"

Corra's mouth fell open as Tayler burst into giggles.

Chapter 13

Corra needed something to take her mind off Chris having fun in Louisville without her, so she decided to take inventory for the gift shop. She picked her children up after school and brought them out to the house with her. Jamie and Katie loved everything about the farm, particularly all the wide-open space where they could run and play and just be kids. As long as they weren't getting into anyone's way Corra let them explore.

She walked into the kitchen just as Rita was preparing her famous lemonade and water with orange slices.

"What are you doing here at this time? Don't the kids have afterschool activities to go to?" Rita asked.

Corra shook her head. "Not today. I came back to take a little inventory."

"Well, grab one of those pitchers, it's tea time."

Corra jumped. "Yes ma'am." She grabbed the pitcher with orange slices and followed Rita into the library.

"So, have you had Chris over for dinner yet?" Rita asked.

Corra bit her lip. "No. Besides, women don't do that anymore. He takes me out to dinner."

"I don't care how much times change, the way to a man's heart is through his stomach. I know you're a good cook. You learned from watching me and your mama."

"Oh, I can cook, we just haven't gotten that far."

"What do the kids think of him?" Rita turned around and went back into the kitchen for platters of cookies. She gave one to Corra. They carried them into the library.

"They like him. But I'm careful about who I bring around them. I don't want them to get attached to him and then he walks out of our lives."

"Chris won't do that."

"What makes you so sure?"

"He's a decent man, from a good family. I know his people. Besides, you two look good together," Rita said with a smile.

Corra blushed and a big dumb grin took over her face. She covered her mouth with her hand.

Rita laughed. "Well now, I've never seen that before. You blushing over a guy."

Corra removed her hand and laughed. "Oh, my God, I can't believe I'm blushing like this. I feel so high school right now." This was the type of conversation Corra missed having with her mother. She walked over and gave Rita a big hug.

By 8:00 p.m. Corra had enough of counting trinkets and boxes. She could be having fun with Chris right now, instead of going cross-eyed in a back storage room. She shut inventory down, turned out the lights, and made her way back over to the house.

Once inside, her cell phone vibrated. She had a text message and stepped into the empty library to see who it was.

Where are you? Chris asked.

At work, she replied. She hadn't seen Chris in a few days, but it felt like months. She missed him.

This late? He asked.

Doing inventory. Plus the kids wanted to see Rollin, Corra responded. Chris didn't respond to her right away, so she kept texting.

Having a good time?

No. He answered quickly.

Corra smiled. She didn't want him not to enjoy himself, but knowing that he wasn't having fun without her was comforting.

I'm sorry, she replied, sincere about that.

Me too.

When are you returning? She waited for an answer, but got nothing. After a moment, she put her phone back in her pocket and sought out her family.

Rita had gone home, and Rollin and the kids were in the family room watching a movie when she walked in.

"Okay you two, wrap it up. Time to go home."

"Mom, can we finish the movie? Please?" Jamie asked from his spot stretched out on the floor.

Rollin appealed to her, "It's almost over. A few more minutes."

Corra concluded a few more minutes wasn't unreasonable. "Okay," she said, and sat down on the couch next to Katie.

At the climax of the movie, her phone vibrated again. She pulled it out to see another message from Chris.

Come out on the front porch.

Where are you? she asked.

On the front porch.

Corra frowned to keep from smiling as she got up and walked from the family room to the foyer. Her heart started pounding in her chest. She opened the front door and Chris stood on the other side. She couldn't believe her eyes.

"Hey, lady."

"What are you doing here?" she asked, as she

stepped out onto the porch. "I thought you were going to spend the weekend in Louisville?"

He leaned in for a quick kiss on the lips. His soft lips sent a shiver through her body.

"I couldn't stand being there without you. Since you didn't want to come with me, I decided I'd rather be with you."

She crossed and then uncrossed her arms, suddenly not knowing what to do with them. "You didn't have to do that."

"I know." He pulled her into his arms for a long, wet and hungry kiss. Then he whispered in her ear, "Can you sneak away with me tonight?"

His kisses were starting to give her brain fog. For a few seconds she couldn't think of what she was about to say. A flashback of them kissing in his pool house came to mind.

Corra whispered, "I don't know, I've got the kids with me."

He reached out and caressed her cheek. "I bet Rollin and Tayler would keep them for you."

She took a step back. "Oh, I know what you're up to." She looked into those grayish-brown eyes of his, peering at her in the dim front porch light. He'd come all the way back just to be with her.

"Let me go check, I'll be right back." Corra knew Rollin and Tayler would have no problem watching the kids. She sought Tayler out and asked her first.

Chapter 14

Corra sat back in Chris's car, nervous for the first time since they'd been seeing one another.

"Did you watch the race?" he asked.

"We did. Did you have the winner?"

He shook his head. "I think my horse is still coming around the track. I've never been good at picking horses. That's why I let you do all the betting at Keeneland."

"Then why did you want to go?"

He shrugged. "It's fun. I used to go every year when I was in school. We'd drive down and hang out in the infield, party hop, drink too much and go home making plans for next year."

Chris reached over and took Corra's hand, intertwining his fingers with hers. Then he brought her hand up to his lips and kissed her knuckles. "Today wasn't exciting at all. All I could think about was you. If you were with me it would have been exciting. Without you, it was just a bunch of drunk overdressed people bumping into one another."

"I'm glad you're back."

He smiled. "You are?"

Corra couldn't hide the overjoyed look on her face even if she'd wanted to. "Yes, I missed you. I haven't seen you since what? Monday. And then you were going to leave me for the weekend."

He shook his head. "It was Tuesday. And I'm sorry, I've been busy renovating my new place. But, you're here with me now."

"Exactly where are we sneaking away to?"

"My place."

Corra's eyes widened. She'd never been to Chris's house in Danville. And she wasn't quite sure it was safe to go home with him. It wasn't him she didn't trust, but herself. She could already feel her body temperature starting to rise.

As Chris drove, he listened to the sweet sound of Corra's voice. He didn't have any plans for the evening. He only wanted to be with her.

Once they reached the house, he pulled into and around the driveway that led down a slight slope to the back of the house. He opened the two-car garage and parked, then cut off the engine and unlocked the doors.

He walked around and opened the door for Corra. They walked up the stairs to the main floor into the eat-in kitchen. Before he'd moved into the house his Realtor recommended an interior decorator who he hired to complete the house. The day he moved in, it was fully furnished and had a homey lived-in feel. He took off his sports jacket and threw it across the couch, then proceeded to give Corra a tour of the house.

"Wow, do you even live here? I mean not a thing is out of place."

"That would be Susan's doing. My housekeeper comes twice a week."

Corra gave him a wide-eyed nod. "You have a housekeeper. No wonder it doesn't have that typical bachelor pad feel. Did you hire a decorator too? Because this looks like something right out of *Traditional Homes* magazine."

He chuckled. "As a matter of fact I did. I don't have a decorating bone in my body."

"Neither do I really, but I would have had a field day decorating this place."

She went on and on about how she would lay everything out. Chris listened to her, but all he could think about was how much he wanted to kiss her. He needed to take her upstairs to his bedroom and make love to her. Every day she walked around in his mind swaying her hips and glancing at him over her shoulders. A tingling sensation ran through him every time she glanced at him that way.

"But I love what your decorator did. This place looks like you. Upscale and manly."

He laughed. "Yeah, that's me all right, upscale."

He remembered he had wine in the refrigerator and hopefully some of the cake his mother baked for him was still there. Once in the kitchen he picked up the remote and turned on the television for background noise. Corra took a seat at the dining room table.

"Would you like something to drink?" he asked, as he pulled out bottles of both red and white wine. He placed them on the counter for Corra to take her pick. The he reached back into the refrigerator and pulled out half a German Chocolate cake.

"Are you trying to put me to sleep?" Corra asked, as she joined him at the counter.

"Not yet." He winked at her before reaching for two wineglasses and a knife for the cake. "My mother made the cake. She's a talented baker, so let me warn you now, one piece won't be enough."

Corra slapped her hip with the palm of her hand. "One piece is all I need. Thank goodness I skipped dessert tonight. I've gained a few pounds since Tracee joined us."

"Well, let me be the first to tell you it's going to all the right places."

"Thank you." She blushed like a teenager.

Knowing he could make her blush made him feel good.

"Which do you suggest?" she asked, pointing to the wines.

He tore his eyes from her for a moment to pick up the bottle of white. "Moscato d'Asti pairs very nice with something sweet." He proceeded to pour her a glass of white wine, but himself a glass of red.

He grabbed two dessert plates and forks. They took their cake and wine over to the kitchen table.

Corra took a bite of the cake and closed her eyes. When she licked the remaining icing from her lips, he wanted to reach over and help her out.

"Umm, this is so good, and moist." Then she took a sip of wine.

Chris did the same.

After a few minutes of talking and eating, he noticed chocolate on Corra's lip.

He leaned closer to her. "You've got something right there," he said, before licking the speck of chocolate from her bottom lip.

Corra smiled. "Did you really just do that? That was a movie move if I've ever seen one."

"Not original enough for ya, huh?"

She laughed. "Not quite. Why don't you try something like this." Corra leaned over and grabbed him by the collar. "Let's see what your cake tastes like."

The moment her mouth met his, warmth flooded his body and the desire to take her became an overpowering need. He wanted her closer. While the taste of chocolate and wine lingered on her tongue, he also detected a longing as urgent as his own. She wanted him.

Corra was pulled into Chris's lap after he opened his legs and turned his chair around. The foreplay they had been engaged in for the last couple of weeks had been enough for her. Chris moaned as they parted lips long enough for her to catch her breath and him to brand her neck with his hot moist lips.

She bit down on her bottom lip as a loud moan escaped. Her heartbeat raced like she was running the Kentucky Oaks herself. Chris worked his way back up to her lips and captured her mouth. She wrapped an arm around his neck as his hand began to caress different parts of her body.

Her body craved this man. A shiver of pleasure ran down her spine when he cupped her breast in his hand. Her eyes fluttered behind their lids and lightheadedness took over. Before she passed out, she broke the hold Chris had on her mouth and threw her head back. She needed air.

"Oh, God. You don't know how long it's been since a man held me in his arms like this," she said.

Corra looked into Chris's eyes and could see what was on his mind. It was on her mind too. No kids. A nice quiet house all to themselves. Did she dare?

Hell yes!

She picked up her glass of wine and stood up. Her eyes locked on his.

A slow smile formed on Chris's lips. He stood, grabbed his wine and took her hand. "Follow me."

She followed him upstairs to the master bedroom where neither of them could wait to get out of their clothes. Chris set the glasses on his dresser. He unbuttoned his shirt while she pulled her top over her head.

Any body image issues Corra may have had before tonight were completely forgotten. She stripped before Chris and her excitement grew as he did the same. Once they were completely naked, standing before each other in their birthday suits, Chris closed the distance between them and engulfed Corra in his arms. His rock-hard body was still that of a football player. His firm arms held her against him while the effects of his erection pressed against her stomach.

She wrapped her arms around his neck and walked backward with him until they were against the bed. As he showered her with kisses he lowered her onto the bed. Corra couldn't believe what was happening, yet she was present and fully aware of it. Her mind was saying "wait a minute," but her body wasn't waiting for anything.

Chris rolled over onto his back and Corra wasted no time straddling him. They stopped kissing long enough for him to make a request.

"Spend the night with me?" he asked, between pants.

She hesitated, then shook her head. "I can't."

"Why not? Rollin and Tayler will keep the kids. Tonight is our night. I want you with me all night."

Corra lowered her forehead to Chris's chest. Only God knew how much she wanted this man. He raked his hands through her hair, pulling it back as it fell on his stomach.

"I've waited a long time for you. And I want to take my time, and love you right."

She sat up and looked down into his beautiful face. He was always well groomed and his olive complexion glistened with perspiration. But, it was the little freckles around his nose and cheeks that turned her on tonight. From her vantage point he was the irresistible, sexy and cocky football player she used to dream about.

With one arm he reached over for the phone on the nightstand, without moving her. He handed her the phone. "Call Rollin. Tell him I'll bring you back in the morning."

She took the phone. "I'll call Tayler."

After the phone call, Chris pulled Corra down until they were chest to chest. He wrapped his arms around her and cupped her derriere in both hands, repositioning her right where he wanted her to be. She was his tonight.

He took his time and caressed, kissed and lavished every part of her body with attention. For the next couple of hours he studied her like he needed to pass an exam. He wanted to find her spot. What turned her on? What turned her off? What drove her absolutely crazy? And what made her cry.

She shivered when he kissed the scar from her broken leg. He pulled a condom from its box in his nightstand drawer. Although he told Corra they had all night, he couldn't wait any longer. His body trembled as he leaned over her. Her lips were parted, and her eyes soft and hungry with desire told him she needed him. She wrapped her legs around his body.

"Make love to me, Chris," she whispered.

He quenched his thirst for her all night long.

Chapter 15

After spending Friday night and Saturday morning with Chris, Corra was all smiles at Jamie's baseball game on Sunday afternoon. She wanted to invite Chris to the game, but he had plans with his father. She missed him already. As she watched the kids run the bases, she could feel Chris's mouth on her breasts and his hands exploring her body. He touched and caressed her in ways that reignited passion she'd suppressed for so long.

Lost in her thoughts, she didn't hear Tayler calling her name until she waved her hand in front of Corra's face.

"Earth to Corra. Are you in there? Or, are you still with Chris?"

Corra shook her head. "I'm sorry, I was lost in my thoughts. I've got so much going on."

"Umm-hum, sure you do. Where's your man this afternoon?"

Corra smiled at how nice that sounded. Where was *her* man? "With his father. He said he'll try to make it next Sunday."

"So how do the kids like him?"

"They think he's the greatest. Jamie's in love with his car."

Tayler laughed. "That boy loves cars almost as much as baseball. He keeps asking if he can drive my car."

A man walking alongside the baseball field caught Corra's attention. Just inside the fence, Rollin threw Jamie a few pitches, helping him warm up. Something they did every Sunday. Jamie was all suited up in his blue-and-white uniform and baseball cap. Corra stood up as the man walked around the fence and she realized who it was. Eric.

"What is it?" Tayler asked, as she stood next to Corra shielding her eyes from the sun.

"What the hell is he doing here?" Corra had not invited Eric to the game.

"Who is he?" Tayler asked.

"It's Eric."

"Eric, as in the kids' father?"

"Yes,"

"He's back from California? When did that happen?"

Corra picked up her purse. She did not want Eric on the field with Jamie. "I'll be right back."

She left Tayler in the stands and headed for the field. By the time she reached them, Rollin and Eric had shook hands and Eric was showing Jamie how to hold his mitt and undoubtedly giving him some baseball tips.

Rollin caught Corra's eyes before she walked up and frowned. He didn't like Eric either.

"What are you doing here?" she asked Eric.

"There you go, buddy, you've got it." He'd taken over playing catch from Rollin. "I'm giving my son a few pointers. You don't mind, do you, Rollin?"

Rollin shook his head. "Not at all. You plan on sticking around for the game?"

Jamie chimed in. "Yeah, Daddy, you gonna stay and watch me play?"

Eric walked over and fussed with Jamie's cap. "I most certainly am. Let's get a little more practice in before the game. Come on."

Corra and Rollin rejoined Tayler in the stands.

"Why didn't you tell me he was back?" Rollin asked.

Corra shrugged. "I don't know."

"Does Chris know?"

She shook her head. "Not that I know of. I know he doesn't like him, but Eric's their father so he's always going to be a part of their lives."

"I hope Eric's not setting them up for a letdown. And if I was you I'd tell Chris."

As the captain called his team in to get ready to

start the game, Eric found his way to the stands. Corra thought he was about to bring his trifling self up there with them, but he stopped short and sat next to a man she now recognized as his old buddy, Dickie. The guy she banned from coming to the house when the kids were small. He was trouble on two legs.

Corra couldn't even enjoy the game. Every time Jamie was up to bat Eric stood up clapping and acting like the proud father. Rollin was the reason for Jamie's baseball skills, not Eric. She tried to ignore him and keep her focus on Jamie and Katie who sat at the end of the bench with one of her little friends. She smiled as they laughed and talked like two old women. Katie had an old, gentle soul.

Sometime before the last inning Eric left. Corra hadn't seen him leave, but when the game was over he was nowhere around.

After dinner with the family Corra returned home to laundry and preparing the kids for the week. Then, Sharon stopped by and they sat around the kitchen table talking.

"You should have seen him sitting there like he was so into the game. If anything he was more of a distraction to Jamie. Poor fella looked as if he was struggling."

"What did Eric say to you?"

"Nothing. Only that he'd come to watch Jamie play. I didn't have anything else to say to him. I just wish he'd had the decency to let me know when he's going to show up. We need to establish some boundaries."

"You still haven't told Chris?"

Corra lowered her forehead into the palm of her hand. "Not yet. I could have kicked myself for not telling Rollin. He was blindsided when Eric approached them."

"Rollin's such an understanding man. Besides, playing daddy is good practice for when he and Tayler have children of their own."

Corra laughed. "And he should be ready with as much practice as he's had over the years. I can't wait until they give me a little niece or nephew."

The doorbell rang, and before Corra could make it to the front door Jamie and Katie came charging down the stairs screaming, "Daddy's here, Daddy's here."

What the hell! Corra looked back at Sharon. "See what I mean?" She turned around and dared the kids to open the door until she got there. When she opened the door Eric grinned at her like he was a young man again who'd come by to pick her up. Only this time she wasn't excited to see him.

"Hey Corra, I thought I'd stop by to see the kids since I'm off this evening."

So he has a job! "Eric, you need to start calling to set things up. How do you know I don't have plans this evening?"

They'd waited behind her long enough. Jamie peeked around Corra. "Daddy, did you see all of my game today?"

Eric squatted down. "I certainly did. My ride had to leave at the very end, but I saw you out there doing your thing. I'm proud of you."

Unable to contain them any longer, Corra stepped aside while Jamie and Katie held the door open for Eric to enter.

He looked up at Corra. "Mind if I come in for a few minutes?"

She shook her head.

Eric waved back out the door at someone parked in front of her house, and the car pulled off. Corra hoped whoever it was had planned on coming back. She wasn't going to take him home.

"That's Dickie, you remember him, don't you?" Eric asked.

With disgust, Corra nodded. "Unfortunately, yes."

Eric shook his head. "He's visiting a friend in the area, so all I have to do is call him when I'm ready. He'll swing back by and pick me up."

She breathed a sigh of relief as they walked up into the living room. "And how long will that be?"

Jamie grabbed Eric's hand. "Come on, Daddy, let me show you what the coach gave us after the game."

"I want to see," Katie said from the other side of Eric, holding his hand.

"Hi, Eric." Sharon stood in the entrance to the kitchen.

He raised his chin. "I see some things never change. You two still best friends?"

"That's right. Corra's my girl. I've always got her back."

"I'll remember that." Eric headed upstairs with his kids.

Corra joined Sharon at the kitchen table.

"I think he's about to become a permanent fixture over here," Sharon said.

"Oh, no he's not. I'll be sure to see to that."

Sharon left an hour later, and Corra was downstairs in the family room folding clothes and watching TV when Eric walked in.

"Where are my kids?" she asked, shaking one of Katie's blouses.

"In their rooms. I wanted to talk to you for a minute."

"Yeah, I need to talk to you too."

"Look, is it okay if I come get the kids this week and take them to the park? There's only so much we can do here."

Corra snapped the next top in the air. "No, it won't be okay. I'm sorry but you haven't been around long enough for me to trust my kids with you."

He sat down on the corner of the couch. "What do you think I'm going to do, kidnap my own kids? I barely have a place to lay my own head."

She folded the shirt and placed it on top of the stack next to her. "I haven't seen you in over two years. And I have sole custody so right now I'm more comfortable if you visit them here at the house."

His jaw tightened, but Corra didn't care. She wasn't ready to let him go off with her kids. She didn't know where Eric lived, where he worked or if he had a dime to his name.

"Okay, I understand. We'll play in the backyard then." He stood up and walked over to look at pictures on the bookshelf. "I didn't realize how much I missed them. Katie's so sweet, I could hold her and never let go. I don't want her to grow up. And Jamie…" Eric shook his head and picked up another picture of Jamie with his baseball team. "He's a remarkable kid. Both of them are." He set the pictures down and turned around to face Corra. "They aren't mad at me. Neither one of them. They keep asking me about my work and why did I have to go away to work."

"Oh, yeah. That's where I told them you were. Out of town on a job."

"How long was I supposed to be there?"

She shrugged. "I didn't know. I knew one day I'd have to tell them the truth, but for now that sufficed. They cried every now and then, but they understood you would be coming back."

"Thank you."

"For what?"

"For not teaching them to hate me after everything I did."

Corra continued her folding. "You didn't try to hurt them, only me. I didn't see a reason to punish them for that."

Eric moved from the couch to a chair across the room. "Corra, I'm gonna make it up to you, I promise. Then maybe one day we can talk about joint custody. I want to spend more time with them."

Corra laughed. "Don't make any promises you can't keep."

"I'm working now, pretty soon I'll have my own place and a car. I'll be able to help you out some. I know it's not easy raising two kids alone."

"My family helps."

"Yeah, well they're my responsibility, not your family's."

Corra stood with her back ramrod straight. That's the first time she'd heard Eric talk about taking responsibility for anything. He was the guy who walked out on his responsibilities. "That's the most grown-up thing I've heard you say, ever."

"Look, I'm gonna call Dickie and get out of here in a few minutes. I'll be upstairs with the kids until he comes."

"Tell them I said to get ready to take a bath. As soon as you leave I'm coming up."

"Okay."

Eric went back upstairs and Corra finished the laundry. Several minutes later, she heard a car horn blow outside. Eric's ride. Dickie probably didn't see anything wrong with sitting out there blowing the horn, but she hated it. She walked to the front door and Eric came down the stairs as she opened the door.

Shockingly, the kids weren't running behind him.

"They're getting ready for their baths, I told them you'd be right up."

Corra nodded. How come kids listened more when a man told them what to do than when a woman did? If she'd told them that they would have ignored her and come running down the stairs with Eric.

"Tell your buddy not to sit out in front of my house and blow the horn, please."

"I'm sorry. You know Dickie. He's a little rough around the edges, but he's cool. I'll make sure he doesn't do it again."

She opened the front door and Eric let himself out onto the front porch. Corra started to step out, but her heart stopped when Chris's silver Cadillac pulled up behind Dickie's car. She had to remember to breathe.

Chapter 16

Chris stepped out of the car, and Corra went weak in the knees. He had a new sexy swag about himself as he walked around the car with his head held high. Her body tingled and craved to be touched by him again.

Eric turned around following her gaze. "Who's this, your new boyfriend?" he asked.

For a moment, she'd forgotten Eric was standing there, until Chris slowed his stride and narrowed his eyes before stepping up onto the porch.

Eric's mouth momentarily fell open. "Ain't this a bitch," he mumbled, before turning back to Corra. "So is this your new man?"

"Eric Hayden, haven't seen you in quite a while," Chris said, holding out his hand.

Eric's eyebrow rose as he stared Chris down, but didn't accept his hand. "Christopher Williams. I thought you moved to New York or somewhere up north."

Chris dropped his hand. "Naw, Philadelphia. But, I'm back in Danville now." He stepped around Eric closer to Corra.

Corra wanted to die right there on the spot. She'd put Chris in such an awkward position by not letting him know Eric was back.

"So what can we do for you?" Eric stood there with his arms crossed as if he lived there.

"He's here to see me. Not that it's any of your business. I believe you were about to leave."

Eric let out a quick disgusted snort before shoving his hands into his pockets and turning away. He lowered his head and Corra thought she witnessed all the fight drain out of him.

Chris stared at Corra with a "what the hell's going on" look on his face.

"Yeah, I'm going, but I'll be back tomorrow." His mouth curled into a sneer as he looked at Chris. "To see my kids."

Chris cleared his throat. "Later, man," he said, before joining Corra in the doorway.

"Yeah, much," Eric mumbled on his way down the steps.

Corra stood back to let Chris in. Her heart was pounding in her chest. She closed the door and followed him up the steps and into the kitchen; the center of gravity for Corra. Everything happened in her kitchen.

The only thing she knew to say was, "I'm sorry."

"What did he do, just show up out of the blue?"

She glanced up at Chris who leaned against the counter. He looked irritated.

"Have a seat, Chris."

He pulled out a chair and sat down.

She took a deep breath. "I heard Eric was back in town so when I ran into his sister, Cookie, a couple of weeks ago I asked about him. Since then, he's come by a couple of times to see the kids." Too nervous to sit down, she fixed herself a glass of water and offered him some, but he shook his head.

"So you went looking for him?"

She shook her head. "Not actually, but yes. If I hadn't ran into Cookie I might not have. Asshole or not, my kids need him in their lives. Especially Jamie. Once upon a time he was a good father." She leaned against the sink and sipped her water.

"Come sit down." Chris pushed a chair out and motioned for her to sit next to him.

Corra was a little nervous about how Chris would take Eric's presence in her life again. But, she also wasn't about to let him come before what was best for her kids. She hoped he understood.

He turned her chair to face him and reached out and caressed her thigh. "Why didn't you tell me?"

"Because I know how you feel about him."

"Corra, regardless of how I feel about him, he's the father of your children. You should have told me. Tonight I didn't know whether you wanted me to leave or stay."

"Stay, of course. I don't want him back after what he's done to me." She lowered her voice. "His gambling and depleting of our finances wasn't the only thing that broke us up. The infidelity with multiple women, coupled with the verbal abuse was the main reason I divorced him."

Chris leaned closer and ran both hands up Corra's thighs. He took a breath, and then let out a loud sigh. "Well, I'm glad I stayed. But, let's not start off by keeping things from each other, okay?"

She smiled. "Okay. And thanks for being so understanding."

He placed his hand behind her neck, leaned in and gave her a kiss. All of Corra's nervousness dissolved when Chris parted her lips with his tongue and slowly set her body ablaze.

Chris released her and leaned back in his seat. "I actually stopped by to see if you had any plans for the weekend."

She shrugged. "No, why?"

"I need a weekend getaway. How would you like to go to Las Vegas with me?"

Corra sat straight up. "I don't know... I, uh, I have to work and I don't have any vacation planned and—"

"And you need a babysitter, and I'm sure you can come up with plenty more excuses. But, I want to take you to Vegas for the weekend."

Corra tried to hide her excitement, but a Las

Vegas getaway sounded wonderful. "Well, I am part owner of the establishment, and I can give myself a few days off. Providing I can get a sitter."

"Great. Work on it and let me know."

"Mom! I'm ready," Jamie yelled, from the top of the stairs.

Chris released her and they backed away from each other, both expecting the kids to run into the room.

Corra laughed and yelled back. "I'm on my way."

Chris scooted his chair back. "I'd better go. I wanted to see you before I went home. How was the game today?"

"It was great. Jamie had two home runs." She stopped short of telling him Eric was at the game. Then felt guilty that she was keeping something else from him. This was no way to start a relationship.

Chapter 17

Tuesday night, Chris joined Corra and the kids for dinner. Corra got the biggest laugh at Chris's face as he tried to keep up with both Jamie and Katie's conversations at the same time. They were like two little people starved for attention. You would have thought they hadn't spoken to anyone in weeks. And Chris ping-ponged from one to the other before stealing a glance at Corra.

He mouthed, "Help."

She laughed. "Okay guys, give Mr. Williams a break. Jamie, you can tell him about the game after you wash up for dinner."

"Are you having dinner with us?" Katie asked, looking up at Chris with a confused expression.

"I was planning on it. Do you want me to stay?"

She smiled and nodded eagerly.

"Okay, young lady, go wash your hands."

Jamie ran upstairs while Katie skipped out of the room at a slower pace, then walked up the stairs.

Chris relaxed back onto the couch and took a deep breath. "Wow, they have a lot of energy, don't they?"

Corra flopped down next to him laughing. "You should have seen your face trying to keep up."

He held his hands out. "Hey, I didn't want to ignore either one of them. So, I tried to give my undivided attention to both of them—at the same time." He shook his head.

Corra leaned over and gave him a kiss on the cheek. "You get an A for effort, Mr. Williams. I have very rambunctious, inquisitive children who will talk you to death if you let them. Jamie more so than Katie."

Chris smiled. "I can get used to that."

Corra loved the fact that Chris was earnestly trying to get along with her kids.

What sounded like thunder was actually Jamie and Katie running downstairs all washed up for dinner. Corra served the kids' favorite, smothered chicken breast with green beans and red potatoes.

Between bites Jamie drilled Chris about everything from playing football with Rollin, to attending another one of his baseball games.

After dinner, Corra cleaned up the kitchen while Jamie entertained Chris by showing off his baseball card collection. The two of them hit it off pretty good. Chris knew a lot about baseball.

Later, the kids retreated to the den and found their favorite television show, while Corra and Chris sat upstairs on the living room couch.

"Thank you for such a wonderful meal. I had a great time tonight." Chris stretched his legs out in front of him.

Corra laughed. "Did you really? I mean Jamie drilled you like you were applying for a job."

"In a way I am. I want to be his mommy's man. I just hope I get the job." Chris leaned over and took Corra's hand in his.

He caressed her knuckles before glancing up with desire in his own eyes. She knew that feeling. "Well, during your first interview Friday night, you performed excellent."

Chris bit the right side of his bottom lip and seductively grinned at Corra. Small palpitations began coursing through her body. Seeing Chris interact with the kids had been like an aphrodisiac. And now, she wanted to take him to bed. But she couldn't.

"You know, one thing I've learned about interviews over the years is that as much as I want the job, the employer has to determine if I'm a good fit or not."

Corra smiled and licked her lips. Chris was baiting her and she loved it. She wanted to be with him again tonight more than anything. She turned on the couch until she faced him straight on. "Mr. Williams. You were a perfect fit."

Chris held eye contact with her as his smile started slow, and then turned into a full-blown ear-to-ear grin. He reached out and pressed his palm lightly against her cheek. "So does that mean I have the job?"

"An offer is being extended."

"And I accept."

Corra's pulse was beating in her throat as the temperature in the room rose. She looked into Chris's eyes. "Welcome aboard."

He leaned over to seal the deal with a kiss.

"Now we really have something to celebrate in Las Vegas."

Corra threw her hand over her mouth. She'd almost forgotten they were going to Las Vegas this weekend.

After Corra said good-night to Chris, she went to give the kids a bath before bed. Katie had fallen asleep in the den in front of the television. Corra carried her upstairs and instructed Jamie to get his bath. As usual he put up a little fight, explaining how he hadn't gotten dirty since yesterday. But, ultimately she won out and he closed the bathroom door.

A few minutes later, the doorbell rang. Corra looked at the bedside clock in her room. It was after eight o'clock and was the kids' bedtime. She hurried downstairs and peeked out the window. Whoever it was had their back to her and kept moving around.

"Who is it?" she asked through the door.

"Eric."

Corra frowned. *What is he doing here at this time of night?* She didn't want to open the door and have the kids hear him. "Eric, it's late and the kids are getting ready for bed. Come back tomorrow."

"Corra, open the door. I need to talk to you."

Shit! "Whatever it is, can't it wait until tomorrow?"

"No. I saw him, and I don't want him around my kids."

She threw the door open. "What the hell are you talking about?"

Corra stepped back as he stumbled through the open door, and quickly tried to right himself. He smelled like a distillery. She'd never known him to abuse alcohol, but clearly he'd changed since their divorce.

Once he steadied himself he looked around. "Where's my kids?" he asked, with slurred speech.

"I told you, they're upstairs getting ready for bed. You've been drinking and I won't let you see them in your condition." She held the door open. "Eric, I'm going to have to ask you to leave."

He looked up at Corra with bloodshot eyes like she was crazy. "I bought this house. If it wasn't for it, that…you wouldn't even be living here."

"*We* bought the house. Then you lost your share in the divorce settlement. So, again I'm asking you to leave." Corra wasn't afraid of Eric. He no longer held any power over her. The only times they'd actually fought were when she caught him with other women.

"I don't want him in here, Corra. He's not taking my kids away from me."

"Eric, what are you talking about?"

"Your boyfriend, Chris," he said, getting louder. "I saw him leaving a few minutes ago. If you let that bastard poison my kids against me—"

"Shhh." Corra glanced upstairs to make sure they hadn't been overheard. Then she turned back to Eric with fire in her eyes. "You've been sitting outside my house watching me?" She was furious.

"I was coming to see my kids, then I saw his car parked out front. So I sat there." He staggered around a bit more trying to keep his balance. "I waited to see how long he was staying."

Corra couldn't believe her ears. He'd been out there drinking and getting madder by the minute.

He pointed his finger in her face. "What you tryna do, replace me with your football hero? You always had a thing for him. Hell, you think I didn't know that."

Corra smacked his hand away. "Eric, leave now."

He chuckled. "I'm not going anywhere." He turned to go up the steps. "Where's Jamie." He called out, "Jamie!"

Corra grabbed him by the arm. "He's taking a bath. Come on, Eric, I'm not playing with you."

He stopped and spun around. His facial expression and tone all softened. He reached out and tried to touch Corra's cheek, but she pulled back.

"I miss you, baby. Didn't you miss me?"

Shocked and horrified, Corra shook her head. "No, I don't."

She pushed past Eric up the steps. "That's it. I'm calling the police."

He reached out to grab her foot, but missed and fell onto the steps. "Okay, okay, I'm going. Just give me a minute. Damn!"

She stood at the top of the stairs with her arms crossed and the cordless phone in hand.

He snickered as he pulled himself up and opened the front door. "I'll be back tomorrow, and your boyfriend had better not be here." He slammed the door on his way out.

Corra lowered her arms and took a deep breath. *What the hell have I gotten myself into?*

Chapter 18

"Oh, my God!" The lobby of the Bellagio Hotel had been the most spectacular thing Corra had ever seen, but this room absolutely took the cake. The huge king-size bed, and the calming indigo and platinum color palette were set off by the breathtaking panoramic view of the Strip. She threw her purse on the bed and walked over to the window.

Chris walked in behind her. "What is it?"

"This view. Is that the Eiffel Tower?"

"Yep, and that's the Paris Hotel across the street." He walked up next to her.

Corra inhaled the crisp cedar-and-sandalwood scene of Chris's cologne. She couldn't believe she was standing next to him marveling at a replica of one of the most famous landmarks in the world. He reached out for her hand.

"Are you okay?"

She wrinkled up her nose. "I'm better than okay."

"How about hungry?"

She smiled up at him. "Starved."

"Me too. Come on, let's find something to eat."

As they walked hand in hand back through the casino to the restaurant, Corra noticed several women check Chris out. She wasn't the only one who appreciated his style. He was fine from head to toe in a pair of long cargo shorts that showed off his toned legs, a designer T-shirt, with a large Tissot sports watch on his wrist.

After grabbing a bite to eat, they dropped a few coins playing slots up and down the Strip, before they returned to the hotel to change into club attire. When Corra stepped out of the bathroom in a short black dress with a deep plunge down the front, and sexy strappy heels, Chris wanted to shout *Damn!* The dress hugged her hips and showed off every fabulous curve of her body. She looked in the mirror and applied more lipstick, then turned around.

"How do I look?"

"Stunning!"

Corra walked over and planted a quick kiss on his lips. He grabbed her around the waist in an attempt to pull her closer to him, but she spun away from him.

"Oh no, mister. I'm dressed now and you're taking me dancing."

Chris smiled. "Can't blame a brother for trying."

He took Corra to TAO, a nightclub in The Venetian hotel where they danced until the temperature in the club forced them to venture out onto the terrace. Chris lucked upon two vacant seats. He motioned a waitress over for drinks.

"Chris, thank you. I'm having so much fun." Corra threw her head back onto the chair.

"And the party's just begun."

"You're kidding, what time is it? I don't think I can party anymore tonight. My feet are killing me."

"Let me take care of that." He turned her chair facing his and reached down for her ankle. He slipped off her sandals and placed her feet in his lap. She closed her eyes as he massaged her feet.

"Oh, God! That feels so good."

"Why do you wear heels if they hurt your feet like this?"

Corra looked up. "Heels make my ass look good, but my feet pay for it."

Chris laughed. "You really do say what you mean, don't you?"

Corra lay back again. "Not all the time. But sometimes I say the first thing that comes to mind. Like it feels like you're making love to my foot right now."

The waitress returned with their drinks and admired Chris's handiwork. "Now you look like a man that knows how to take care of his woman," she said.

"I most certainly do," Chris said as he smiled at Corra.

She bit her bottom lip as she remembered him taking very good care of her last Friday night. Enough with the foot foreplay, she was ready for the main course. She picked up her drink and took a sip without taking her eyes off Chris.

He looked at his watch. "Getting sleepy?" he asked.

Corra shook her head. "Too excited to sleep."

He lowered her feet and picked up his drink. "That makes two of us. But it is after one and I've been up since six."

Corra frowned. "Party pooper."

"Never," Chris said with a shake of his head. "I've just got another party in mind that takes place at the Bellagio."

Corra didn't even finish her drink, nor did Chris. The desire to be with him reached a boiling point. When he helped her up from her seat, he held her in his arms and kissed her. The kiss was hot and deep, but he pulled away before she lost herself.

He took her hand and led her back through the club, down the Strip and into the Bellagio. They kissed some more as they waited for the elevator.

Chris opened the door to their room and Corra strutted past him to the window, drawn by the lights on the Strip. He closed the door and met her at the window. From behind, he wrapped his arms around her and lowered his head to kiss and nibble at her neck. She raised her arms and wrapped them around his neck.

With Chris at her back and that magnificent view in front of her, Corra opened up like a flower. His hands slid down to the hem of her dress, pulling it up until his thumbs captured her panties—pulling them down.

She shimmied her hips as her panties fell to the floor. She stepped out of them, then turned around facing Chris.

"You won't need those at this party," he said, lowering his voice to a whisper.

A shiver ran through Corra's body, and she swallowed hard.

Chris took his suit coat off, and threw it across the room in a chair. "You look gorgeous tonight, but this dress has to go." He caressed her shoulders and arms.

She held her arms up as he pulled the dress over her head. Tonight she'd let him seduce her. Or was she going to seduce him? She stood totally naked as she reached out to unbutton his shirt. He helped her, then took over until he was completely naked. She smiled thinking that this man was hers.

Neither spoke a word. He reached out and caressed the side of her cheek, running his thumb across her lower lip. She closed her eyes to enjoy the moment, then felt his mouth replace his thumb. He kissed her and she returned the kiss as if she hadn't been kissed in a decade. She tasted the liquor on his breath, and smelled his familiar scent that she wanted all over her body.

His hands caressed their way around her body and down her back until his palms settled over her butt. Warm blood flooded through her body as he turned the temperature up with every touch. He lifted her up and she wrapped her legs around his body, and her arms around his neck. Still devouring her mouth he carried her over to the bed and gently laid her on her back.

He smiled, looking down at her. "Let the party begin."

Corra arched her back and squirmed in anticipation. Chris's head lowered to her stomach where he planted sweet kisses all over her stomach and breasts, stopping to suckle on each nipple. She shivered from his light touch.

He stopped and looked up into her eyes. "Are you cold?"

She shook her head. "No. It just feels good."

Chris lowered himself and lay beside Corra, pulling her close to him. "I remember wanting to hold you in my arms like this all the time. When I used to see you around town I wanted to ask you out, or to run away somewhere with me."

Corra laid her head on Chris's chest as he held her. "I wish I'd known. But you were never without female companionship, so how could I have known."

"Things aren't always what they seem."

"What do you mean?" Corra asked.

"How does that song go, when you can't be with the one you love, love the one you're with. You asked before why I never said anything about my feelings for you. I could have stood up to your father and brother, but back then I felt inferior to just about everybody in town."

Corra pushed herself up on one elbow and looked Chris in the eyes. Those beautiful grayish-brown eyes stared back at her with a sadness she'd never seen before. "Why?" she asked.

"In my eyes everybody had more than we did. Financially, socially, emotionally, you name it. Rollin was my best friend, and I envied him. He had the type of dad I wanted to have. He never treated me like he had more than I did. I didn't want to jeopardize that. I wasn't interested in half of the women I found myself with."

Corra slowly shook her head. Words escaped her at the moment. She lowered her head and kissed Chris's chest.

"You married Eric so I moved on, but I never stopped wanting you. You were the only one for me."

With tears in her eyes, Corra pushed herself up and straddled Chris. The lump in her throat prevented her from speaking, but she didn't need words.

The desire in his eyes said it all. With a hand behind her head he pulled her face closer to his and engaged her in a deep passionate kiss that she didn't want to end. The kiss was filled with so much passion and desire it brought tears to her eyes.

Chris wanted to enter her now, but he had all night. He was going to take his time and savor every spine-tingling moment. He hadn't meant to bare his soul to her, but the words came tumbling out after all these years. A weight had been lifted from his chest.

He removed his hand from her neck and placed both hands on her hips as he rocked her against him. Her thighs were warm and smooth against his skin. When she sat up to catch her breath, he almost lost his. He admired her beautiful breasts while the moisture between her legs coated his manhood. It was almost too much to bear. He strained to hold off a little longer.

He moved his hands from her hips to her breasts, caressing them as the throbbing between his legs intensified. She moaned as she rocked her hips over him then arched her back offering her breast to him. Before he exploded, he reached down to lift her, sitting her a little higher in the middle of his stomach. She leaned over, offering her breast for him to feast upon.

While he kissed and sucked her breast, he ran his hands down her back to her buttocks and squeezed. The searing heat between her legs subsided as she pulled her legs together and he wrapped his arms around her, managing to flip them over until he was on top. Then his hands moved inside her thighs, spreading her legs farther apart. He slid his fingers inside of her to see just how ready she was.

Chapter 19

Corra squirmed beneath Chris as his fingers entered her while his hot mouth continued to feast on her breast. The heat stirring inside of her intensified as she gasped for air. She needed him to make love to her now. She wanted to remove his hand, flip him back over, and ride him until she'd given him everything she had to offer.

Chris released her breast and moved up to plant small kisses all over her face. He ran his hands across her thighs, spreading them wider, then stroked between her legs. She came up off the bed as her breath caught in her throat. He stopped kissing her and stared down into her eyes as he continued to pleasure her with his hand.

Breathless, Corra said, "Chris, don't. I want to feel you inside me."

He stopped. Corra closed her eyes and took a few deep breaths as Chris climbed off the bed and back on in a matter of seconds. She looked down and he had a condom package in his hand. His enormous erection waited for him to rip the package open.

She sat up and reached out, taking his hard and smooth erection in her hand. He stopped and lowered the package from his mouth. He looked down at her hands around him and moaned. They were both trembling and panting as Chris cupped his hand behind her head and brought her mouth to his lips.

Corra held Chris tight within her hands. He moaned through his heavy breathing while she caressed him. He must have dropped the condom package because he held her face in the palms of his hands and devoured her mouth. She stroked harder and faster until he rose up on his knees. Then his body went rigid before he pulled away from her.

"Oh, you're killing me," he said in a raspy, hoarse voice.

"In a good way I hope," she whispered back.

"In a wonderful way," he whispered, before he reached down and ripped the condom package open. He rolled it over his stiff, enormous shaft, then looked down at Corra with smoldering eyes and a hard-set jawline.

She lay back, opening her legs, welcoming him to her. With one quick thrust he was inside. She gasped and wrapped her arms around him while her body adjusted to his size. She closed her eyes and tried to breathe, as he filled her to capacity. Once he started taking her, she wrapped her legs around his body and held on for dear life. Corra loved every minute of their lovemaking, their love sounds and their love faces. He took her hard and fast at times, then slowed down to cool her off with kisses to her neck and mouth. She squeezed him as tight as she could inside of her which produced small cries from his lips before he plunged deep inside her again.

Corra thought she'd pull her hair out, sex with Chris was so good. He knew when to withdraw slowly and when to go deeper, thrusting to give her everything he had. She matched him thrust for thrust, feeling the fire inside her build until she thought she would explode.

She cried out. "Oh, Chris! Yes!"

He responded with, "Oh, I love you, baby."

Then he covered her mouth with his and hungrily, greedily, plunged his tongue inside as he found his release. He groaned and grinded inside of her as Corra's body shuddered beneath him finding her own release. For a few minutes, she was in heaven.

Afterward, she loosened the grip her legs held around his body, but didn't want to let him go. He buried his face between her neck and the pillow and tried to regain his breathing.

She lay there with stars dancing around behind her eyelids. Slowly she returned to earth. Chris kissed her neck a time or two before taking a deep breath. She kept her eyes closed while aftershocks plagued her body. His hot body lay on top of her moving ever so slowly with the aftershocks. She ran her hands down to his buttocks and squeezed, holding him there.

He eased up on one elbow and gazed down into her eyes. His pupils looked dilated and the edges of his mouth slowly turned up in a grin. "What are you doing?"

"Holding on."

"May I ask why?"

"Because I don't ever want you to come out."

He laughed and lowered his face into the pillow. Corra joined in laughing at herself.

Once the laughter subsided Chris whispered in her ear, "Baby, I don't want to come out either, but give me a few minutes and I'll be back." His lips found hers again.

A few minutes later, Corra lay in Chris's arms, her body limp and completely satiated. Euphoria after sex was so foreign to her. He brushed her hair back from her moist forehead and kissed her there.

"Did I hear you say that you loved me?" she asked.

"You heard that, huh?"

"Uh-huh. Did you mean it?"

Chris traced Corra's face with his eyes, so intense and serious. Then he smiled.

"I think you know I've been in love with you for as long as I can remember. When I came home last year and you asked if I could help with the fundraiser, I can't tell you how excited that made me.

Just being around you again made me realize I had to have you."

"And then we had the accident."

"I'm sorry I wasn't here to help with your recovery. But after what we just did I'd say you're fully recovered."

Corra laughed and tapped him in the chest.

"Baby, I mean you had your legs wrapped around me in a locked position. I thought we were remaking a Prince video of 'International Lover' or something."

Corra threw her head back and laughed loud enough to wake anyone sleeping next door. She hadn't had a moment of stiffness or anything remotely related when Chris made love to her.

"I love it when you laugh. It's like you release everything inside of you and just let loose. Laughter is good for the soul."

"Yeah, but I haven't had a good laugh like this in a long time."

"Your life should be filled with laughter."

She sighed. "My life has been filled with responsibilities and work. Not much room for laughter."

Chris didn't say anything for a few minutes. Corra laid her head on his chest and listened to his heartbeat.

"Corra, a couple of weeks ago when we were talking you mentioned that Eric had been abusive to you. In what way?"

Corra's body tensed. Talking about her ex again wasn't something she wanted to do tonight. But, since he'd bared his soul to her she needed to clear the air.

"He never hit me, but he was verbally abusive. I think it made him feel good to belittle me when things weren't going good in his life. He wouldn't go to church or anywhere else for counseling. Instead, he sought refuge in other women. After a while, he started saying things in front of the kids. That's when I decided I wouldn't take it anymore."

"Nobody wants their marriage to end in divorce, but I'm happy you left him. If you hadn't we might not have been able to reconnect."

Corra smiled up at him.

"I'm not an abuser of any sort. All I want to do is love you. Like I said before, you're the only one for me."

Around three o'clock in the morning, Corra straddled Chris for the second time and they made love again until the point of near exhaustion.

After a late breakfast Saturday morning, Corra and Chris went shopping up and down the Strip. She purchased Las Vegas trinkets for the kids, and Chris let her pick out a new pair of sunglasses for him. When they approached a designer shoe store, Corra remembered Tayler's Jimmy Choos she'd admired so much. She had to take a walk on the wild side and venture inside. Chris followed her and helped her pick out a nude stiletto that she modeled around the store for him.

"I like the way those make your calves look,"

Chris said, as he leaned over and ran his hand down Corra's calf and ankle. He glanced up at her. "They're sexy as hell. Do you like them?"

She held her foot out and twisted it from left to right, admiring how well the shoes fit, and how comfortable they were. She sat down and took them off, holding one shoe up. "God yes! I love them."

Chris looked up at Savannah, the most patient salesperson Corra had ever met, and said with a smile, "I'll take them."

"Excellent choice," Savannah said, with a wink at Chris.

Corra's breath caught in her throat as Chris took the shoes from her and handed them to Savannah. She'd only wanted to see if they were comfortable, since they were quite pricey.

"Chris, I can't let you do that. Those are—"

He stood up and cut her off. "Corra, I'm a big boy, you don't need to let me do anything." He nodded for Savannah to go ahead and ring them up. Then he turned back to Corra. "You deserve beautiful things like those shoes and more. And I want to give them to you."

She quickly stepped back into her shoes and stood to meet him face-to-face. "Chris, if this is because of last night I won't accept them." She lowered her voice. "You don't owe me anything."

He took a step back and stared at her. "Is that what you think I'm doing?" He didn't wait for an answer. "I want you to have those shoes. It has nothing to do with the love we made last night."

Corra crossed her arms. Was he trying to make her feel cheap?

Chris closed the distance between them and wrapped his arms around her. "Corra, if I could buy you happiness and the solutions to any problems you ever have in life I would. But I can't. So don't deprive me of giving you something that makes you feel good."

He released her and ran his hands down her arms. He placed a gentle kiss on her lips. "Let me love you in every way I know how, okay?"

She lowered her arms and blinked several times to keep from crying. She never thought she'd find a man who would buy her expensive shoes and be good to her kids, something she'd laughed with Tayler about. But, here he was standing right in front of her. "Just don't spoil me. I might learn to like it."

Chris laughed. "Trust me, you're gonna love it."

Saturday night, Corra wore her new shoes to dinner. The sway of her hips and the new confidence in her stride, all compliments of Jimmy Choo and Chris Williams. She even had a little luck at the roulette table after dinner.

The elevator crawled up to the fourteenth floor, testing Chris's patience. He hadn't been able to keep his hands off Corra all evening. Now he wanted her in nothing but her heels.

He opened the door to their room and took Corra by the waist as she crossed the threshold. His hunger for her was insatiable. His lips met hers before he could close the door. She giggled and lay her body against his as she wrapped her arms around his neck. He sucked and kissed her lips before picking her up and walking over to the bed. She tossed her purse across the room in a chair.

When he let go of her she lifted her ankle behind her and reached down to unstrap her shoes.

"Eh, eh, don't take them off." He whispered in her ear, "I want to make love to you with them on."

Everything about Corra drove Chris wild at the moment. Her scent, which had been enticing him all night. Her giddy, appreciative attitude had made him want her all night. And now the opportunity to live out one of his fantasies with her consumed his mind.

She whispered back at him, "Chris, you're so nasty."

He gently pulled on her bottom lip with his lips. "You haven't seen nasty yet. Turn around." He helped her spin around and held her arms up so he could unzip her dress, which zipped up the side, and help her out of it. He tossed it over on the chair with her purse.

He kissed her neck, shoulders, back, anywhere his lips could reach while he held her breasts in the palms of his hands and gently massaged them. Corra responded in a way that let him know she was all his.

He ran his hands over her hips and eased her black, barely there, bikini panties down. She stepped out of her panties and he tossed them with her other things. He took a step back. The view from behind was intoxicating.

Corra glanced back at him over her shoulder. Holding the corner of her bottom lip between her teeth, she looked like a woman waiting to be fucked.

He quickly stripped, then ran his hand up her back and leaned forward. "Bend over, baby. I want it from behind tonight."

Corra was the perfect lover. She did what he asked all night long. This was their last night in Vegas, and he made sure it was one she'd never forget.

Chapter 20

Two weeks later, on Memorial Day weekend, Chris took Corra, Jamie and Katie to Beech Bend Amusement Park in Bowling Green, Kentucky, to celebrate the end of a successful school year. The kids and Chris loved the excitement of the rides, and Corra loved to watch them.

She especially enjoyed the look on Chris's face as he stepped off the Dizzy Dragon, a contraption she refused to get on. He gripped Jamie and Katie's hands, but she wasn't sure who was holding who up.

"Mom, Mom, did you see that?" Jamie urged as he hurried toward Corra, pulling Chris along. "We went real fast."

"Having a good time?" she asked Chris, who looked a little green around the gills.

He took a deep breath. "I'm having a ball, but I think I left my stomach back there on that ride."

The kids laughed and begged Chris for another round.

Katie tugged on Chris's arm and looked up at him, which shocked Corra. "Mr. Williams. Will you do one more with us?"

Chris shared a smile with Corra. "You with us this time?"

How could she say no? Her kids had taken to Chris even with Eric being back in their lives. Chris was good to her, and the kids. She loved him. "Okay, one ride."

"Oh, I know!" Jamie let go of Chris's hand and held his arms up to get everyone's attention. "Let's do the haunted house. Please Mom, please."

Corra had never, and would never go into the haunted house. She shook her head.

"Please Mom, please," Jamie and Katie sang out in unison.

"You know I don't do stuff like that," she said.

"Why not?" Chris asked.

"She's scared," Jamie volunteered.

Corra wanted to pop him in the mouth for revealing her secret. But, he was right, she was scared.

"It's not that. I just don't do dark, unfamiliar places."

Chris laughed. "Come on. The ride seats four. You can sit next to me, and the kids will be right in front of us."

"Come on, Mom. Please." Jamie and Katie started in again.

"Okay, okay, I'll go."

Chris grinned and reached out for Corra's hand. "Don't worry. I won't let anything happen to you."

Corra and Chris walked hand in hand with the kids in front of them skipping along and talking excitedly about the haunted house.

"Thank you," Corra leaned over and said to Chris.

"For what?" he asked.

"For indulging the kids and showing them a good time."

"It's my pleasure. Besides, I love amusement parks. Some rides more than others. And the haunted house is my favorite."

"How on earth can that be your favorite?"

"You'll see."

The anxious knot in Corra's stomach grew as they stood in line waiting for their turn to be tortured. By the time they reached the front of the line her palms were sweaty, and she had difficulty catching her breath. Chris squeezed her hand tighter before pulling her in for a hug.

"Relax, you're with me. I won't let anything happen to you."

His words sounded reassuring, but she didn't like spooky. Especially the kind that lurked, waiting in the dark.

For what seemed like eternity but was more like ten minutes, the kids alternated between jumping and laughing, while Corra practically sat in Chris's lap. She was petrified every time something popped out. Chris wrapped an arm around her and laughed every time she screamed. The minute their cart broke through the black doors into sunlight again Corra let out a deep breath. Her body was still pressed against Chris's and now she knew why this was his favorite ride.

The minute they walked away from the ride Jamie grabbed Chris by the arm. "Can we go again?"

Before Corra could protest Katie grabbed her hand. "Mom, I need to use the bathroom."

"I'll tell you what. While the ladies go to the restroom, how would you like to try the Kentucky Rumbler?" Chris asked Jamie, but immediately looked at Corra for approval.

She tilted her head. Jamie had ridden the roller coaster before with Rollin, whom she trusted her kids' safety to. And it wasn't that she didn't trust Chris with her son, it was more like she was afraid to have him out of her sight.

Jamie recognized the apprehension on her face, and started pleading. "Can I, Mom? Please, please, please."

"Why don't you wait until we come back?"

"Corra, I'll guard the little man with my life. I promise you we'll be okay. By the time you guys leave the restroom we'll probably still be standing in line. Go ahead, we'll be okay." Chris leaned over and kissed Corra on the cheek, then whispered in her ear, "Trust me. I won't let any harm come to him."

So she did. While they ran off to get in line for

the roller coaster, she escorted Katie to the restroom. Like herself, Katie wasn't very fond of roller coasters.

After the Kentucky Rumbler the four of them sat down to eat lunch, and then rode a few more family-friendly rides before calling it a day. Corra hadn't seen her kids this happily exhausted in a long time. Katie was so tired Chris carried her back to the car. They slept all the way home.

"Did you have a good time today?" Chris asked, as he drove down the highway.

Corra stretched as best she could from the passenger seat. "Yes. I haven't had this much fun in quite a while. Thanks."

"You don't have to thank me. I think I needed today just as much as they did. I haven't rode that many rides, or ate that much junk, in years. It was fun."

"Yeah, I could tell you were enjoying yourself. And I think my kids are in love with you."

Chris laughed. "The feeling is mutual. They're great kids. I just hope their mother is in love with me as well." He reached out for Corra's hand, brought it to his mouth and kissed her knuckles.

"Oh, she is. Even more so."

Chapter 21

Tuesday morning on Chris's drive into work his father called and informed him he needed to get out to his house. Something had gone wrong with the renovations.

Chris turned his car around and gunned it out to the house. He came to a grinding stop just behind the police cruiser that sat parked right in front of the property. His father's car was in front of the police vehicle.

From the outside everything looked fine. But the minute he opened the front door his jaw set. At first glance, he could tell someone had taken a hammer to the banister because of the way it practically lay on its side. He closed the door behind him and followed the voices coming from inside the kitchen. He jumped when he stepped on what sounded like broken glass. He looked down and the floor was covered with small shards of glass. The original Schonbek chandelier was hanging in pieces. He closed his eyes and cursed under his breath. The rest of the damage couldn't be worse than that.

Inside the kitchen, his father, Brian the contractor, and local officer Greg Mason stood discussing the atrocities surrounding them. Greg, an old classmate, turned around and shook his head as Chris walked in.

"Chris, your father was filling me in on what happened out here." Greg offered his hand.

They shook hands as Chris noticed the broken kitchen window. "Great, maybe somebody can tell me what happened."

Brian walked them through the house explaining that everything was intact when he left last night, and he hadn't seen anybody suspicious this morning. Vandals had punched holes in the walls, spilled paint onto his hardwood floors and destroyed just about anything else they could get their hands on inside the house.

Nathaniel stood at the foot of the living room steps looking from the broken banister to the trashed chandelier. "Kids and those damned drugs. Don't they have anything better to do than to destroy other people's property? Just look at that banister! It's an original work of art. Destroyed. And the Schonbek, it's irreplaceable."

As mad as Chris was, he now realized that most

of the damage was superficial and could easily be fixed. He walked over and patted his father on the back. "At least no one was here when they came in. That means more to me than all this stuff."

"Chris, there's probably some teenagers behind this, but I have to ask, do you have any idea who would want to do this?" Greg asked.

Chris shrugged. "No. But, with kids being out for the summer, maybe they get a kick out of trashing vacant houses."

"I don't know, we haven't had any cases like this in quite a while," Greg said.

A lightbulb went off in Chris's head and he snapped his fingers. All attention turned to him. "Eric Hayden and I had words a few weeks ago. He's moved back here."

Greg nodded. "I ran into him a couple of weeks ago myself. We've been keeping an eye on him. What were your words about?"

"I'm dating his ex-wife."

"Corra Coleman?"

"Yeah."

Greg took a deep breath. "Yeah, I can see that getting him riled up. And from what I remember you two never did get along very well, did you?"

"You have a good memory," was all Chris said.

"Well, I'll check him out. You don't mind if we take a few pictures for the report, do you?"

"No, not at all. Do whatever you have to. Just find the bastard responsible for this."

* * *

A couple of evenings later, Corra and Chris were strolling through Fayette Mall in Lexington, and Corra couldn't believe her eyes. Walking toward them was Kyla with her arm looped around a young man. Kyla had always been so into her studies and dedicated to her projects that Corra had never seen her with a man before. So Kyla wasn't all work and no play after all.

Chris stopped at a kiosk in the middle of the mall to examine some glasswork as they approached.

"Hey, Kyla," Corra called out to get her cousin's attention.

Kyla gave Corra a double take, before releasing the young man's arm and bringing a hand to her chest. "Corra!"

A tentative smile covered Kyla's face as she looked startled and at a loss for words.

Corra made the first move and walked over to say hello to Kyla's friend. The look on Kyla's face was priceless.

While the three of them chatted, Chris joined them. Kyla introduced her friend as a former classmate who lived in Lexington. In the middle of their conversation, Corra was distracted by Chris peering across the crowd. She followed his gaze. A few stores down Eric glared back at him with a cocky grin on his face.

To her dismay, Eric and some anorexic-looking woman started toward them.

Kyla was saying something, but alarm bells were

going off in Corra's head. She touched Chris's arm to get his attention, and felt how tense he'd become. When he turned to her, she noticed his flared nostrils and the hardened look of his face. Was it that serious?

"Chris, are you okay?"

He nodded. "I'm fine." Then he turned back and glared at Eric as if he were daring him to enter their space.

Kyla followed Chris's gaze. "Who's that?" she asked, as Eric approached.

"My ex-husband, Eric."

"Oh, yeah. I remember him."

In a faded LeBron James T-shirt, cutoff long shorts and sneakers, Eric strolled up to them.

"Hey, how's everybody doing?" Eric asked, smiling in Corra and Kyla's direction.

"Hello, Eric." Corra greeted him without an ounce of enthusiasm.

Eric gave Chris a quick head nod. Chris didn't nod back.

Eric introduced his lady friend, then Corra introduced Kyla and her friend. Of course, Eric didn't remember Kyla. He probably didn't remember most of her family members since he hadn't participated in any of her family functions. Chris didn't say a word. His intense stare at Eric said it all.

"Where are the kids?" Eric finally asked.

"They're at Rollin's," Corra said.

Eric's date tugged on his arm, ready to go. He said something to her and then turned back to Corra. "I've got something for Jamie so I'll see you later tonight." He cut his eyes up at Chris once more before walking away.

"Well, uh, I'll catch you guys later," Kyla said, as she and her friend walked away.

Corra and Chris said their goodbyes, then Corra turned to Chris. "What was that all about?"

"What do you mean?"

"The staredown between you and Eric. You looked at him like you wanted to hurt him. I know you don't like him, but you could at least be civil."

Chris looked at Corra with furrowed brows. "Be civil to a man who leaves his family without paying any child support, returns to town without looking them up, and then expects to just walk back into your life."

Corra narrowed her eyes. If they weren't standing in the middle of the mall, Corra would have smacked Chris.

"We've had this discussion. He's around for his kids, that's all."

Chris ran a hand across the top of his head in frustration, and took a deep breath. "I know. I'm sorry. Come on, let's go."

He walked away, but Corra didn't move. His dislike for Eric ran deep, and if they were going to continue their relationship she needed to know what it was about.

Chris stopped when he realized she wasn't following him. He turned around and came back. "What's wrong?"

"You tell me? I've never seen you this upset before."

He took a deep breath. "I don't like that his presence does this to us."

Corra's head snapped back. "His presence infuriates you, and I need to know why."

Chris looked around as several people had given them more than a moment's notice. Corra didn't care. If Chris had a violent streak, she wanted to know now.

He put his arm around her shoulder and said softly, "I'm sorry. I shouldn't have let him get to me. The last thing I want to do is fight with you." He kissed her on the lips.

They stood there as the crowd walked around them.

"I don't want to fight with you either, especially about Eric. So, let's forget about him and go home." She wrapped an arm around his waist and they continued through the mall. She still planned to find out what had happened between them two.

Chapter 22

After breakfast Friday morning, Corra and Tayler agreed to help Kyla test her research project for her Ph.D. She'd prepared a program to teach students about organic farming. Her nonprofit program started with a summer camp, then a school-year educational program she hoped to have in place next year. Rollin's farm hands had helped build her an open-air-style classroom setting. All around her were organic plants and flowers from the gardens. Currently, the only staff she had were the farm's two interns from the University of Kentucky.

Corra and Tayler chatted while Kyla prepared to start.

"The big day is less than a month away now, how do you feel?" Corra asked Tayler.

Tayler took a deep breath. "Excited, elated. Nicole's flying down with her fiancé, who I can't wait to meet. My family's traveling from Chicago, and we'll all be staying under one roof. I'm excited about them seeing the place."

"Yeah, I'm pretty stoked myself. I'm so happy for you and Rollin."

"What are you so happy about?" Rollin asked, as he walked up behind them.

"Oh, I've got that." Kyla dropped what she was doing and ran over to help Rollin with two large pails full of flowers.

"I'm happy you guys are getting married in a few weeks and I'll have a sister-in-law."

Rollin set the flowers down and walked over to Corra and Tayler. "That's right, in a few more weeks you'll be Mrs. Rollin Coleman," he said, as he leaned over and planted a kiss on Tayler's lips. "I've got you now. There's no getting away."

Corra smiled watching her brother and Tayler's touching display of affection. Tayler held his face in the palms of her hands and kissed him. They were so perfect for one another. Their wedding was going to be beautiful and she would probably cry from the beginning until the end.

"If you need anything else just come find me," Rollin told Kyla. "Oh, I almost forgot Reverend Daniels has us scheduled for a rehearsal this Sunday after church."

"Sunday! But what about Jamie's game?" Corra said.

Rollin shrugged. "Will it hurt to miss one?"

"Let Chris take him," Tayler suggested.

"Chris?" Corra hadn't thought about him.

"Yeah, why not. You said they've been bonding. What better way than to bond over a game of baseball. I hate to miss the game too, but this is the only time Reverend Daniels has."

Corra had to admit it was a good idea. Her kids loved Chris. Every time he came around they did something fun. Be it a movie night, or an ice cream run, they enjoyed his attention.

"You know, that is a great idea. I'll give him a call to see if he's free. Or, brave enough."

"Sounds like a plan," Rollin said before he kissed Tayler again, and went back to work.

"You guys are beautiful together. I'm so glad you came to stay here when you did," Corra shared with Tayler.

Tayler smiled. "You and Chris are beautiful together as well. I think you're going to be next."

Corra laughed. "Huh! I don't know about that. Yesterday, we ran into Eric in Lexington at the mall. Chris looked at him like he wanted to kill him. I don't know what transpired between them two but I can't have that. What if Jamie or Katie were around?"

"Did you ask him about it?"

"Yes, but he didn't really tell me anything. He's never liked Eric."

"Maybe Rollin knows. Have you asked him?"

"No, but they're so buddy buddy, he might not tell me."

"Blood's thicker than water. Ask him about it."

Kyla joined them, ready to start class. "Ladies. I want to thank you for helping me. This is the first trial run of my summer teaching program."

After Kyla's class Corra ran across Rollin on her way to open the gift shop. "Rollin, I need to ask you something."

He wiped the sweat from his forehead. "Sure, what's up?"

"Why does Chris dislike Eric so much?"

"Why don't you ask Chris?"

"I did. He won't tell me."

Rollin pursed his lips together and shook his head. "Corra, I'm sorry, but you're gonna have to ask him. I can give you two reasons why I don't like him."

She rolled her eyes at Rollin. "How come I knew you'd say that? You guys stick together."

"It's not like that. You're my sister, so I wouldn't keep anything from you that I thought would hurt you. If something happened between them, I'm not aware of it."

"Yeah, well I'm afraid they're going to get into a fight one day. You should have seen the way they stared each other down the other day."

"Chris is a grown-ass businessman, he's not going to get into a fistfight with Eric."

Corra nodded, thinking about the look on Chris's face. "I certainly hope not."

Sunday after church, Chris picked Jamie up and took him to his baseball game. He was excited about having some alone time with Jamie. So excited, he wore a matching baseball shirt and hat. Jamie had to be the coolest ten-year-old Chris had ever met. Katie stole his heart every time they were together, but today she chose to stay with her mother.

"Are you excited about today's game?" Chris asked Jamie.

If Chris hadn't glanced at him he never would have noticed Jamie nodding his head. He sat quietly in his white-and-blue uniform. His glove was nestled perfectly in his lap.

"How many more games do you have before the season's over?"

"Three more. And, we might make it to the championship. If we win today, and next time."

"What do you think your odds are?"

Jamie beamed. "Nobody can beat us. We only lost one game this season."

"Impressive. Are you any good?"

"I'm the second best on the team. My friend Ronnie, he's the best kid on our team. On any team."

"Oh, man. Do you want to play baseball when you grow up?"

Jamie smiled and shrugged. "I don't know."

"Haven't given it much thought, huh?" Jamie started to fidget around in his seat like he'd put him on the spot.

"I'm gonna be a dog doctor," he finally said.

"So you like dogs?"

"Yes, but my mom won't let me have one right now. She said when I get older we can get a dog."

He was ten. Chris wondered what Corra was waiting on. "A dog's a lot of responsibility. Are you ready for that?"

"Yes. And my daddy said he's gonna get me a dog."

"He did?"

"Yes. He said I can keep it at his house. When I go over there I can play with it."

"Have you been over to your daddy's house?"

Jamie shook his head. "He don't have a house yet." The tone of his voice rose as he found a subject he wanted to talk about. "He comes over all the time and teaches me how to play baseball. He likes baseball just like you do."

Chris glanced out the window as they pulled up to the ballpark. "Yeah, I'm sure he does."

"Do you know my daddy?" Jamie asked.

"I do. We used to play baseball together a long time ago." He put the car in Park and killed the engine. He smiled at Jamie. How could this bright kid be a product of Eric Hayden's?

Chris sat in the stands and cheered like some proud papa. Jamie was good. He reminded Chris of himself when he was young and finding his footing in sports. By the sixth inning Chris noticed Jamie bent over, hands on his knees, trying to catch his breath. He was on second base looking to steal third, when something went wrong.

Slowly, Jamie leaned forward and collapsed over the plate. Chris jumped to his feet. The coaching staff rushed out to second base. Chris's heartbeat raced as he took the bleachers two at a time until he reached the fence. Jamie sat up trying to catch his breath, with the help of his coach. Chris's throat swelled with fear. An image of Corra who'd trusted the care of her baby to him flashed though his mind.

Chris ran around the fence onto the diamond, running out to Jamie's aid. Somebody yelled, "Call an ambulance."

Chris quickly let the coach know Jamie was in his care. He kneeled down beside him and noticed the perspiration on his face and the strained way in which his chest rose as he fought for his breath. That scared Chris to death.

"Does he have asthma?" the coach asked.

Chris shook his head. "No, not that I know of. I mean his mother never mentioned it."

"I've never known him to have it either," the coach said before someone handed him a piece of paper to fan Jamie with. "Everybody get back and give him room to breathe." Everyone took a step or two back, except Chris.

"Jamie, do you have an inhaler?" Chris asked.

Jamie shook his head. The look of fear in his eyes tore Chris apart. He had to do something other than wait for an ambulance. He stood up and rushed over to the crowd of parents. "Does anybody have an inhaler? An asthma inhaler?"

Everyone shook their head. "Is he having an asthma attack?" someone asked.

"I don't know, but I think so." Chris continued around the baseball diamond before he returned empty-handed.

Jamie sat up next to the coach, breathing a little better, but still having difficulty. The coach looked up at Chris. "Let's get him over to the dugout." He kept his hand in the middle of Jamie's back rubbing and comforting him.

Chris tried to remain calm as he took Jamie's other arm and walked with them.

"He just needs to stay calm until the ambulance gets here."

"Forget the ambulance," Chris said. "Let's get him over to my car and I'll take him to the emergency room myself." Chris's legs and hands were shaking as they passed the dugout.

Chris glanced up briefly to see a group of men coming across the field toward them.

"What's wrong with him?" A loud baritone voice came at them.

Eric Hayden and a few of his thuggish friends caught up with them. Chris glanced at the coach who diverted his eyes down to Jamie.

"I think he's having an asthma attack," the coach offered.

Eric stopped in front of them and kneeled down to Jamie. "You okay, son?"

Jamie took more panting breaths and shook his head.

Eric stood up and turned his anger toward Chris. "What did you do to him?"

Chris opened his mouth to tell Eric to get out the way so he could get Jamie to the hospital, but the coach beat him to it.

"Jamie collapsed on second base. The ambulance hasn't shown up yet so Chris is taking him to the emergency room. Do you know if he has asthma?"

Eric looked dumbfounded. "Not that I know of." Then he gave Chris another dirty look. "Where's Corra? Or Rollin?"

"Wedding rehearsal. Look, Eric, we can discuss all this later. I need to get Jamie to the hospital right now."

"*You* need to get him to the hospital? Get your hands off my son. You're not taking him anywhere." Eric reached out for Jamie's arm.

Chris put his hand out to stop Eric. "Look, Corra left him with me. I'm taking him to the hospital. You can follow us, but get out of my way."

Eric's eyes widened. He glanced over his shoulders at his buddies who looked like they were ready for a fight. "Did you hear that? I can follow *him*." Then he turned back to Chris, who along with the coach had moved aside and attempted to keep walking with Jamie.

Eric held out his arm to stop them. "That's my son! If anybody's taking him to the hospital, it's me." He took Jamie from the coach and another guy reached out to take his other arm from Chris.

"Somebody just get him to the hospital," the coach yelled. Chris reluctantly let go. As much as he hated to admit it, Eric was Jamie's father. "I'll be right behind you," Chris informed Jamie.

"Have you contacted his mother?" the coach asked Chris.

Chris released a stream of curse words as he watched Eric and his friend place Jamie into the back of a car and speed off. He paced around as he pulled out his cell phone. "Not yet. I'm calling her now." His stomach hardened into a knot as he waited for Corra to answer.

This was the hardest call he'd ever had to make. As the phone rang he gripped the back of his neck and continued to pace around in short spans. He really screwed up. He could feel it. He hadn't handled the situation right.

"Hello?" Corra's hurried voice came from the other end.

Chris could tell from her tone she already knew something was wrong. He knew of no tactful way to tell her so he blurted it out. "Corra, Jamie had an asthma attack or something and he's on his way to the hospital."

"What! Where is he?"

Chris could tell from her breathing that she was about to start panicking. He froze.

"Chris, where is my baby?" she screamed.

After a deep breath Chris found his voice. "Eric is taking him to the emergency room. He was having difficulty—"

"Eric! What is Eric doing with him?"

"Corra, calm down. He showed up as I was—"

"Don't tell me to calm down. Where are they? I don't want him alone with my baby. He doesn't have custody or any right to take my son."

Chris's chest tightened. He bit his lower lip and

cursed himself for not knowing how to handle this situation.

"Chris, find my baby. I'm leaving here right now."

He tried to say something else, but she hung up on him. He ran to his car, jumped in and took off for the emergency room at Ephraim McDowell. He prayed Jamie would be okay.

Twenty minutes later, Chris paced around the waiting room, furious to have learned that Eric dropped Jamie off and left. Seconds later, Corra and Rollin burst into the room.

Corra rushed up to Chris. "Where's my son?" she asked.

"They've taken him back for observation, and the nurse needs to see you." He pointed Corra toward the nurse station. Chris didn't want to waste another minute apologizing again, she needed to see Jamie.

Rollin hung back. "What happened?" he asked.

Chris took a deep breath. "Jamie passed out on second base. The coaching staff ran to his aid. He was having trouble breathing. Does he have asthma?"

Rollin shook his head. "No. At least he hasn't shown any signs of it before."

"Well, he looked to be in the middle of an asthma attack." Chris explained everything that happened at the ballpark. After he told Rollin about Eric taking off with Jamie he realized himself he never should have permitted that.

"Man, I know Eric's his father, but Corra doesn't trust him." Rollin looked around. "Where is he? Back there with Jamie?"

Chris shook his head. "The bastard took off."

Rollin's head snapped around. "What?"

"When I walked in the nurse informed me Jamie was here, but that the man who brought him in left. Said he'd be right back, but he hasn't shown up." Chris looked down at his watch. "And I've been here for almost thirty minutes now."

Rollin patted Chris on the shoulder. "Thanks, man."

Chris walked over and took a seat. "For what? Corra's mad as hell that I let Eric take Jamie. I should have known better."

"Don't beat yourself up. Let me go check on my nephew. I'll be back."

Chris couldn't help thinking he'd just screwed his relationship with Corra. After today, she probably never wanted to see him again.

Thirty minutes later, Rollin emerged from the emergency room and rejoined Chris in the waiting area. Chris was determined to wait until Jamie was safe before he left the hospital.

"He's going to be okay," Rollin assured Chris. "The doctor says he's developed a case of asthma. He's going to contact Jamie's physician and suggest some treatment. He's breathing normal now."

Chris exhaled a sigh of relief. "Man, you don't know how good it feels to hear that. I was praying for the little guy." After a beat he asked, "How's Corra?"

"Nervous, scared, you name it. She'd noticed him having a little breathing problem before, but never anything that amounted to an asthma attack. She had no idea he had a touch of asthma. Right now, she's hovering and afraid to let him go."

"Man, I could kick Eric's ass. Why didn't he just let me bring Jamie over here? How the hell does a man take his son to the emergency room and just disappear? And why didn't I insist on taking him myself? After the shit he's done to me I never should have allowed him."

"What shit?" Rollin asked.

Chris shook his head, not really wanting to discuss it, but he knew Rollin would understand. He took a deep breath. "A couple of weeks ago Eric and I had some words. I'm sure seeing me with Corra pissed him off. Then a few days later somebody broke into the house I'm refurbishing and trashed the place. I can't prove he did it, but I'm pretty sure he did."

"You think he'd do something like that?" Rollin asked.

Chris tilted his head toward Rollin and gave him a skeptical look.

"Man, he's too old for that kind of stuff. I'm assuming you called the police?"

"My dad did. Greg was there when I got to the house. He's looking into it, but with no evidence or proof of any sort, it just looks like some kids did it."

"Which is possible," Rollin added.

"Yeah, but Corra and I ran into him in Lexington a few days later and he stared me down like he was daring me to say something. He did it, all right. I'm just not sure how I can prove it. And even if I could, should I press charges?"

"Did you tell Corra about the house?"

"No, I can't prove anything, so I just left it alone. No major structural damage was done. Besides, I've patched it all up and installed some security cameras."

"You know, I love my sister to death, but Eric has always rubbed me the wrong way. The other day she asked me about the bad blood between you two."

Chris ran his hands down the front of his pants and shook his head.

"Hey, I'm not trying to get into your business. You know how I feel about that. But, he's a part of the kids' life, and if you're going to be a part as well, I think you and Corra need to have a talk."

Chris knew Rollin was right. He only hoped Corra would speak to him again. Over the next couple of hours Tayler showed up with Katie, Jamie's coach came by, and a few of his teammates. Everybody came and went, but Chris wasn't going to leave until he spoke to Corra. She hadn't come out yet, although he'd called her cell phone and sent her a text message.

Rollin tried to get Chris to leave. "Look, man, you might as well go on home. I'll come back and pick Corra up once the doctor releases Jamie."

Chris shook his head. "I'll tell you what. Why don't you let me take them home once the doctor releases them? You don't have to let Corra know I'm out here."

Rollin turned to Tayler who nodded her head. "Let him. They need to talk."

"Okay, but look, if she gets mad and refuses, give me a call. I'll come and get them."

Chris patted Rollin on the back. "Thanks, man. I'll take care of them, you know that."

"I know you will. And if that no good-for-nothing ex of hers shows up—"

"Don't worry." Chris cut him off. "I won't make the same mistake twice."

Chris and Rollin gave each other a hug before he left.

Chapter 23

Corra called and texted Rollin twice, letting him know Jamie was being released from the hospital, but he hadn't contacted her back. As the nurse wheeled Jamie out into the lobby, Corra tried once more. Where was he? She was beginning to get concerned. The minute she stepped into the lobby, Chris walked toward them. Her body stiffened as she took a step back. Unfortunately, right into Jamie and the wheelchair.

"Mom!" Jamie yelped, as Corra almost sat in his lap.

"I'm sorry, baby." She caught herself while still holding the phone waiting for Rollin to answer. She asked the nurse to excuse her for a second, and turned away to leave Rollin another voice message.

While Rollin's voice mail message played she heard Chris talking to Jamie. "How's my little buddy feeling?"

Rollin's greeting ended. "Rollin, where the hell are you?" she whispered into the phone. "They just released Jamie and we need a ride home. You said you would be here." She sensed the presence of someone standing behind her.

She disconnected the call and closed her eyes for a moment knowing that Chris was behind her. She was so mad at him she didn't trust herself not to curse him out.

"Corra. Come on, let me take you and Jamie home."

She whirled around and glared at him. "No thanks. We'll wait for Rollin." She took a firm stance and crossed her arms.

Chris had taken Jamie's wheelchair from the nurse. The two of them looked cute in their baseball outfits. Corra had never seen them dressed alike. She bit down on her bottom lip. No matter how cute they looked she couldn't forget the danger he'd potentially put her son in.

"Watch this, Mom." Jamie gave Chris the signal and he pulled the chair back, popping a wheelie. Her son laughed so hard, Corra had to smile. Her baby was going to be okay.

Chris stopped the chair next to her. "Ready to go?" he asked.

Corra looked at her phone.

"He's not coming," Chris said. "I told him I'd take you guys home."

Corra lowered her arms and said through clenched teeth, "I should have known the minute I saw you. Wait until I see him."

"If you're going to be mad at anybody, be mad at me. I told him I wasn't leaving until they released you guys. I just want to make sure you get home safe."

It was almost one o'clock in the morning, what choice did she have? As much as she hated to admit it, at the moment she trusted Chris more than anyone, besides Rollin.

She nodded, and followed Chris and Jamie out to his waiting car. Chris had pulled his car close to the emergency room door. He helped Jamie into the backseat and held the door open for her. A nurse waiting behind them took the wheelchair back.

Minutes into the drive, Jamie fell asleep in the backseat. Corra hadn't uttered a word until now. "I don't know what made you think it was okay to let Eric take Jamie anywhere."

"Because he's his father."

"But I have sole custody of my kids. All Eric can do is come see them at my house."

"With the way you've been letting him come around how was I supposed to know that?" Chris glanced in the rearview mirror, which made Corra peek back to confirm Jamie was still asleep. He was snoring.

"I know how you feel about him, but he's their father, as you've pointed out to me on numerous occasions. I know now it wasn't the right thing to do, but at the moment, it seemed like the only thing I could do."

"Yes, I want my kids to know their father. But, Eric's been out of our lives too long for me to trust him alone with my kids. He willingly gave up custody. And you see what he did tonight." On fire, she glanced out the window into the darkness and shook her head. "He just left him there."

Jamie coughed, getting Chris's attention, as he stirred in the backseat. "Can we talk about this after we get Jamie home and in bed?"

"Not tonight. I'm too upset to talk." Corra relaxed her head back onto the headrest and closed her eyes. She knew Chris didn't have much experience with children, but she expected better from him. All she wanted right now was to be home alone with Jamie and Katie.

Corra must have dozed off as well, because when the car pulled into her driveway, it jolted her awake.

"What the hell is he doing here?" Chris said.

Corra sat up to see a car parked in front of her house with the passenger door open and Eric sitting on her front steps.

She wanted to race out the car and run over and smack the hell out of him. Even worse, she wanted to kick him where it hurt for leaving her baby alone at the hospital. The only problem was, Chris wouldn't allow it.

She pulled on the door handle, but nothing happened.

"Corra, hold on." Chris reached out and touched her arm.

She jerked away from him. "Unlock the door, Chris." All Corra could see right now were her hands around Eric's neck. She wanted to cause him bodily harm.

"Let's get you and Jamie inside, I'll talk to him."

"He doesn't need a damned talking to, he needs his ass kicked." She pulled up on the door handle again. "Take the child locks off."

"I'm going to take them off, but I want you to get Jamie and go in the house."

"Is that Daddy?" Jamie asked. He was awake now and looking out the window.

"That's the...yeah, that's him," Corra spat.

Jamie went to open the back door, but Chris stopped him.

"Hold on a minute, little man. You just got out of the hospital, let me help you out there." Before he released the child locks, he turned and gave Corra a "don't do it" look.

She heard the locks pop and threw the door open. She walked around the back of the car to Jamie's side and opened the door. He was totally capable of getting out of the car himself, but she helped him anyway. Chris stood next to her, closing the door after them.

Corra held Jamie by the back of his shirt. She could tell he wanted to run to his father, but the look of Eric sitting on her steps talking to himself and holding what looked like a bottle of beer between his legs scared her.

"Come on, let's get you inside," Chris said to Jamie.

As they walked toward the steps, Eric stood up, leaving the bottle along the side of the steps. Corra turned Jamie's head.

"Well, well, if it isn't Mr. Christopher Williams. Here to take what's mine once more."

The streetlight in front of Corra's house revealed Eric's bloodshot eyes. Chris ignored his comment.

"Jamie, you all right?" Eric asked, and tried to reach out to him as soon as they were close enough.

Corra took Jamie by the shoulders and turned him away from Eric. "Don't touch him. Not after what you did tonight."

"What I did! I took him to the hospital. Your boyfriend here didn't know what to do."

Chris stepped between them. "Look, Eric, why don't you go sleep it off and come back tomorrow. You don't want the kid to see you like this."

Eric took a step back. "Like what?"

Chris held Eric off while Jamie and Corra hurried up the front steps. "Hey, man, is there somebody you can call to come get you? You don't need to be driving tonight."

"I drove over here, didn't I?" Eric walked around Chris. "Corra, baby, I need to talk to you."

"Eric, go home," Corra said over her shoulder before opening the front door and rushing inside.

Chris pulled out his cell phone. He couldn't let Eric drive in his condition.

"Who you calling, the police?" Eric asked, looking back at Chris.

"No, a cab. You're drunk."

"The hell I am. So what I had a few beers. Then I come over here to see how my boy is and nobody's home." Eric sat down on the step and pointed at Chris. "But, once they showed up I knew you'd be with them. Know how I knew that?"

Chris didn't answer him.

"Because you're a thief. You always have been. You stole everything that ever mattered from me. You really want to be me."

Chris stepped over into the grass and looked up at Corra standing in the doorway. She'd walked out just in time to hear Eric ranting. The door made a squeak and Eric turned around. When he saw Corra he stumbled to his feet.

"Baby, look. I've been trying to show you that I'm a changed man. I can take care of you and the kids again. Just give me a little—"

Chris turned away and gave the cab company instructions on how to get there, then hung up. He wasn't going anywhere until Eric was off Corra's property.

"Are you kidding?" Corra's voice rose several octaves as if she'd forgotten it was after one in the morning. "You just showed me how much you want to be a father, by deserting your son. He was scared to death. What the hell is wrong with you?"

Eric started up the steps again. "I'm, I'm, sorry. I was coming back." He stopped and pointed at Chris. "I was looking for him. He done something to Jamie. He ain't never had no asthma before. Not until he took him to the field. And where were you? Why did you leave Jamie with him? I'm his father, not him."

Corra walked to the top of the steps and lowered her voice. "In the last couple of months, Chris has been more of a father to them than you have. Don't play the good father with me. I had to hunt your ass down just so they would know you were alive."

Chris hoped the cab would get here soon. He hated to see this play out on the front porch like this, but then he didn't want Jamie to witness any of it either. Until the cab arrived he realized he had to defuse the situation. He walked up on the porch and tried to ease Corra back into the house.

"Corra, come on, it's late. You can have this discussion another time. Jamie's inside alone and a cab is on the way to pick Eric up." To his surprise she backed up with him until she was standing inside the storm door.

"So you're gonna let this asshole take my family from me? Take my kids from me?" Eric pleaded as he stepped up onto the porch.

Chris hated to see him try to gain sympathy from Corra. "Man, why don't you go sit in your car until the cab comes." He tried to take Eric by the arm and usher him down the steps, but he pulled away from him and stood with his shoulders back, defiantly.

"You are not gonna take my son away from me."

"I'm not trying to take Jamie or Katie from you. But I do love them and their mother. I want what's best for them. Look, man, I know you're hurting, you don't want your son to see you out here behaving this way. When the cab comes, go home, sleep it off, tomorrow you can sit down and explain what happened to Corra." *Tell her why the hell you left your only son alone at the hospital.*

"Just let you have them, huh? Like you took my baseball career away from me."

Chris's head snapped back as if he had been struck.

Chapter 24

"Eric, I didn't take anything from you. You got hurt junior year when you collided into me on the field, it was an accident. Then you quit coming to practice. You expected the coach to keep you on the team when you weren't showing up? You weren't going to qualify for a sports scholarship because you needed to be more responsible. You need to man up and finally face the facts."

Chris knew he'd hit a nerve when Eric lumbered up his shoulders and neck as if he was ready to throw a punch. Why had he let Eric goad him? This was the last man Chris wanted to get into a fight with.

No matter how much liquor Eric had ingested, Chris knew he'd never throw a punch. Weakness was another of Eric's flaws.

Corra opened the door and stepped out onto the porch. "What the hell are you two doing?"

Having her attention gave Eric more courage. "That's bullshit, man. You took the one thing from me that I wanted more than anything. That hit you gave me on the field was intentional, and it side-lined me. You weren't better than me. You never have been."

Corra threw her hand up trying to calm Eric down. "I don't believe it. You're arguing over some high school shit! This is crazy."

Chris realized something for the first time tonight. Eric envied him. Not just because he'd come into Corra's life, but his resentment went all the way back to high school. He blamed Chris for him not having a successful baseball career. All the years of rude-ness, sneering at him, and talking negatively about his mother in high school, was his way of dealing with losing his position to Chris.

There were no words that could change what happened years ago, but Chris understood Eric better now. For Chris, his position on the baseball team was just another sport to excel in. For Eric, it may have been his future.

Corra and Eric kept arguing until Chris stepped back in. "Eric, I'm sorry, man. I never meant to take anything away from you. If baseball meant to you one tenth of what football meant to me, then I'm truly sorry."

At first Eric frowned at Chris. Then he started laughing and wagged his finger at him.

At the same time, a taxi cab pulled to a stop in behind Eric's car.

"You're good. I guess you think that apology is going to make up for everything." He pointed to Corra. "This is what you want? A thief."

"Oh, Eric, go home. I've had enough. Get in the cab and go."

Eric applauded. "Bravo, Mr. Williams. You win tonight. But don't think for one minute I'm giving up on what's mine."

Chris didn't say another word. Instead, he walked out to the taxi and instructed the driver to take Eric wherever he wanted to go. He slipped him the money without Eric noticing.

With a little coaching from Corra, Eric staggered down the steps, closed his car door which was still open, and slid into the back of the taxi.

After the cab pulled off, Chris walked back up on the porch.

"If he causes you any trouble when he comes back for the car don't hesitate to call the police. I doubt that he will, but just in case."

"I will." Corra stood inside the storm door.

Afraid to speak, Chris looked into Corra's eyes hoping to see relief that he'd gotten rid of Eric for her. Instead, he saw narrowed eyes, locked and loaded, and aimed right at him.

"Thank you for the ride," she said, her tone sharp.

"Sure. Will I see you tomorrow?"

She looked away. "I don't think that's a good idea."

He nodded. *Okay, so she needs a little time to think about it.* "Sometime this week then?"

"Chris, I've got a lot on my plate with the upcoming wedding and all. Maybe it's best we do our own thing for a while."

He tilted his head. *What the hell did that mean?*

After a two-week setback, the contractor finally finished Chris's house. The interior decorator he hired completed the final touches a few days later, just in time for a reporter to come out and take pictures for the local paper. His first guests, as promised, were his family. He gave them the grand tour, pointing out how he'd preserved so many of the historical interior details.

"Oh, Chris. This is simply amazing." His mother, Dakota, stood in the foyer admiring the new traditional Schonbek crystal chandelier.

His mother's pain level was a three today, which made Chris happy. Dakota insisted on taking the stairs by herself. Nathaniel and Pamela followed them.

"See the intricate carvings on this banister?" Nathaniel ran his hand along the wood as they went upstairs. "I worked on that for hours, getting it just right."

Chris shared a smile with his mother.

In the master bedroom, Pamela opened the balcony doors and walked out. "Wait until Darlene sees this place." She stood against the railing with her arms spread out wide and yelled, "Look, Ma, I'm on top of the world!"

Chris laughed, then playfully closed the doors on her.

After the tour and lunch, the women were eager to explore the property more, while the men kicked back by the pool.

"Son, I don't mean to be nosy, but what happened to the Coleman woman with the two children?"

Chris took a deep painful breath and leaned back in his chair. "She's not speaking to me right now."

"Why not?"

Chris replayed what happened Sunday night two weeks ago. Since that night he hadn't slept well, nor been able to fully concentrate on anything. He'd let Corra down. In the weeks that followed, he'd put all his focus on completing the house.

"Don't beat yourself up. I know you had plans for your future that included them."

"How do you know that?" Chris asked.

"Because, I had kids of my own. Your guest rooms upstairs are painted for a little boy and a girl. And I've never known a man who needed a shoe closet. Just have faith that God will bring them back to you."

Nathaniel smiled, stood up and patted Chris on the back. "Don't give up on love, son."

Chris stared out into the pool while his father joined the women inside. He now owned the largest, grandest home in all of Danville, which was exactly what he'd always wanted. So why wasn't he happy about it?

* * *

"Corra, that dress is stunning." Sharon zipped up the back of Corra's dress. Corra stood in front of her bedroom mirror staring at her knee-length, lavender, chiffon halter bridesmaid dress that was perfect for the July heat.

She was so excited about Tayler and Rollin's wedding she had to model the dress again for Sharon.

"So what shoes are you wearing?" Sharon asked. "You need something sexy, yet simple. You don't want to take away from the dress."

"I don't know, but I'll find something by next week. Time is running out."

Sharon rummaged through Corra's closet pulling out shoe after shoe. "Oh, my God! These are amazing." Sharon held up Corra's Jimmy Choos.

Corra reached out and gently took the shoe from her friend. The minute she held it, she remembered the last time she had them on. The memory brought a smile to her face. She held the shoe against her chest.

"Those are the shoes Chris gave you, aren't they?" Corra nodded.

Sharon got up from the mound of shoes around her and walked over to sit on the edge of Corra's bed. Corra followed her with her back to Sharon so she could unzip the dress.

"Don't you want to try them on to see how they look with the dress?" Sharon asked.

"I don't need to. They're perfect. Get me out of this dress before I start crying all over it."

Sharon unzipped the dress. "You haven't had them on since you came back from Vegas, have you?"

Corra shook her head and wiggled out of the dress.

"Then you definitely need to wear them. They're fabulous."

"But Chris gave them to me and he'll be there."

"Good. Maybe seeing him again will bring you to your senses. That man is the best thing that's happened to you since Katie was born. And I know. I've listened to you complain about the quality of men you've met over the years. Corra, Chris was good to you. So he made a mistake. No man's perfect."

"He made a big mistake."

"Yes, and I'm sure he's apologized a thousand times. Come on now, you said yourself he was bonding with the kids. And Eric's been spending quality time with them since the incident as well. All's well that ends well, right?"

Corra hung her dress up and changed into a pair of shorts and a tank top. "Sharon, you don't have any children, do you?"

Sharon crossed her arms. "What's that supposed to mean?"

"If you did you would understand the level of fear I went through that night. Something I never want to feel again." She turned off the closet light and closed the door.

Corra followed Sharon out of her bedroom. Down the hall Sharon stopped and turned around.

"You know, I may not have any children, but I

wouldn't be so stubborn that I couldn't recognize a good man for my children when I saw one. A man who's everything I've ever wanted." She turned back around. "But then again I don't have children, so what do I know."

A lump formed in Corra's throat. The constructive criticism she dished out is what she valued most in her friend.

Sunday afternoon, everyone showed up for Jamie's last baseball game. Corra was overwhelmed by the support. Before the game Rollin threw balls with Jamie as he'd done all season. There was no sign of Eric, or Chris. Not that Corra expected to see Chris, but deep down she had hoped he'd show up.

When Jamie came up to bat Corra sat on the edge of her seat. His doctor had diagnosed him with intermittent asthma, which if treated properly could be controlled. She cheered when her baby hit a home run. It didn't look like his asthma diagnosis was going to keep him out of the game.

After the game, the team celebrated at a local ice cream shop. Corra and Katie joined them. In the middle of the celebration, Jamie came over and sat with them.

"Mom, do you think Chris was at the game?" he asked.

She shook her head. "No, honey, I didn't see him."

"Is he ever coming back?" Katie asked, holding her ice cream cone up to the sky.

Corra closed her eyes. She'd done the one thing

she had no intention of doing. She'd brought a man into her life, introduced him to her kids, and now he was gone. Her stomach churned with disgust. She set her cup of ice cream down. How the hell could she have done that?

She leaned back and put her arms around her kids. "You like Chris, don't you?"

Both of them nodded vigorously.

"He took us to Beech Bend Park," Katie announced.

"Well, he's pretty busy with work right now."

"Like Daddy was?" Jamie asked.

After a deep breath Corra decided to come clean. "No, not like your daddy. Chris owns a company here in town, and sometimes he gets real busy. So he might not be coming back to see Mommy again for a while. But, he'll be at the wedding next week and you can see him then."

"Yippee!" Katie cheered.

"Did you break up with him?" Jamie asked.

Corra looked at her little man with new eyes. He was growing up. "Something like that, yes."

Chapter 25

Corra stood in Rollin's bedroom on the most important day of his life, almost in tears. "This is the perfect weekend for a wedding. The weather is beautiful, the house is immaculate, and the whole family is here."

"Only two people are missing," Rollin added. "I wish Mama and Daddy were here."

"Yeah, me too," Corra agreed.

"I think I miss them more today than I ever have," he said, staring at himself in the mirror.

"Don't make me cry." Corra wiped at her eyes. "Are you nervous?"

He seemed to consider the question for a moment, then shook his head. "Nope. I'm confident I'm marrying the right woman."

Rollin pulled on his suit coat and gave himself one last look in the mirror.

"So handsome," Corra said. "Tayler's a lucky woman."

"Don't I know it," Rollin said, as he bounced up on his toes.

Corra punched him in the arm.

"I'm just playing. If anybody's lucky it's me." He turned to Corra with a serious expression on his face. "And thanks for helping me see that. I know I can be kind of stubborn sometimes."

She smiled. *Looks like that runs in the family.*

Rollin turned around and wrapped his arms around Corra. "In case I haven't told you lately, I'm so proud of you. I know it's not easy raising two kids by yourself on the salary I can afford to pay you."

"Thanks, but like I told you, this house is our family legacy. I wouldn't want to work anyplace else. I'm amazed by how much we've grown since last year. And the future looks brighter than ever."

The bedroom door opened and Rollin released his embrace. Corra wiped at the tears welling in her eyes. Her single brother was about to be a married man. Hopefully, one day Jamie and Katie would have more cousins.

Rollin's best man walked in. "Oh, isn't this touching. Brother and sister sharing a moment." He closed the door behind him and walked over to give Rollin some dap.

Corra smiled. "Well, I'll let you two do what guys do while I go find my sister-in-law."

After making a quick pass through the family quarters to make sure everything and everyone was okay, Corra worked her way through the guests. Finally, she reached the stairs. Since the staircase would be a major focal point of the ceremony, earlier that morning Kyla and Corra had decorated it with tulle and flowers. If she had to say so herself, they did a stunning job.

Inside the same bedroom Tayler once occupied when she first arrived in Danville, Corra found her and her family. Corra had met Tayler's family the day before, when they arrived, and instantly liked them.

"Oh, my God, Tayler! You look stunning." Corra stood with her mouth open admiring Tayler in a white fitted gown with spaghetti straps, detailed with beaded lace, crystals and a small train.

Tayler smiled. "Me! You look amazing. And I see you have your Jimmy Choos on." Tayler pulled up her dress to show off her shoes.

"Silver stilettos with wings?" Corra burst into laughter. If she knew Tayler those shoes cost a fortune. "Where did you get those?"

"Compliments of my husband-to-be. A good man buys you shoes."

Seconds later, someone opened the door and said, "Showtime!"

Corra could hear soft music coming from downstairs. With her emotions running high, she walked to the door, but quickly turned around to give Tayler a gentle hug, and whispered into her ear, "Welcome to the family."

* * *

After posing for too many pictures to count, Corra made her way into the backyard reception filled with beautiful flowers and beautiful people. Young men from their church served as waiters. The church had also loaned them a large tent that covered most of the area, along with some extra chairs. Guests floated in and out of the house.

While Corra and Tracee were admiring all of their hard work, Kyla and her date stepped out into the backyard, holding hands.

"That's the same guy I saw Kyla with at the mall. Is that her new beau?" Corra asked Tracee.

"Looks like it to me, but she said they're just friends."

"I think somebody's coming out of her shell."

The couple walked right past Jamie and Katie who stood several feet away talking to Chris. During the ceremony Corra tried like hell not to glance in his direction, which was hard since he sat on the second row. He'd looked as handsome as always in a beige summer suit.

Now, he'd shed the jacket and tie. The kids pointed at her and pulled him in her direction. She turned her attention back to Tracee, who'd chosen that very moment to go back inside.

"Mommy, look who we found," Katie said. Chris pretended to let the kids pull him.

"Mom, Chris said I could go for a ride in his car," Jamie declared.

Corra gave him the evil eye. No matter how many

times she asked that boy to stop pestering people about their cars, he never would. The minute he was old enough to drive she was going to have her hands full.

Chris smiled at Corra. "Hey, how you doin'?"

She smiled back. "Great." Seeing him again set off the butterflies in her stomach. Memories of their lovemaking replayed in her mind as she looked at him.

"You look great. I like the shoes," he said, with a smile.

When he purchased them he'd said they looked sexy on her. "Thank you." She bit her bottom lip, thinking about how much they'd turned him on.

"Mom, can I go for a ride in Chris's car?" Jamie asked again.

"No. Stop asking me that. And leave Mr. Williams alone."

Jamie let go of Chris's hand and with a pout, crossed his arms over his chest. A group of little girls walked past and Katie disappeared with her new friends.

"So, I'm Mr. Williams now?" Chris asked Corra.

She hadn't even realized she'd called him by his last name. "That's what they should call you, you're an adult."

Chris gently gripped Jamie by the shoulder. "Jamie, why don't you look for me in a few minutes, and if your mother approves, I'll give you a spin down the road before I leave."

Jamie uncrossed his arms. "Oh, boy. Can I, Mom?"

Corra looked up at Chris and shrugged. "I guess it's okay."

Elated, Jamie turned to run off. "I'll be back in a few minutes."

"You're leaving so soon?" Corra asked.

"Unfortunately yes, I'm flying to Philly later."

"Duty calls." She smiled and gestured with her fist.

Chris smiled and momentarily glanced down at the ground. "Yes, it does." After a beat he said, "I finished the house."

Corra's eyes widened. "Congratulations! I'm impressed."

"Thanks. Maybe you and the kids can come out for a pool party before the summer's over."

"Sure. Maybe."

She waited for him to apologize again. When he didn't, she wondered if she should.

A few people passed and spoke while Corra tried to avert Chris's stare. He was polite, but never took his eyes off her for long. The minute they were alone again she found herself wanting to usher him inside the house away from everyone so she could have him all to herself. She wanted them to stand naked holding one another the way they did the first time they made love. She wanted to make love in her Jimmy Choos again.

Chris looked at his watch. "Well, I'd better be going."

"But the reception's just starting. You're not going to wait until they cut the cake?"

He shook his head. "Everything's beautiful, by the way. I know you did a lot of the decorating."

"Thank you." The wind went out of Corra's sails knowing that Chris was about to leave. Sharon had been right, Chris was a good man.

"Oh, is it okay if I give Jamie a spin around the block?"

She took a deep breath. "Sure, just try not to get into an accident."

He laughed. "I'll try my best not to. Enjoy yourself. I'm going to hustle over and say goodbye to the bride and groom."

No! Stop! Don't go! Everything in Corra wanted to ask Chris to stay. She wanted to apologize for her behavior. Couldn't they just pick up where they'd left off? Instead of saying anything, she just stood there feeling sad and lonely as he walked away.

Chapter 26

The start of the new school year found Corra more prepared than she'd ever been. She made pancakes, bacon and eggs for Jamie and Katie who sat down for breakfast before school. Their backpacks were by the front door, and their lunches were packed and waiting for them at the end of the counter.

"Mom, can we go to the park after school today?" Katie asked.

"You most certainly can, right after you finish your homework. So that means you do what as soon as you come in from school?"

"My homework."

"That's right. Jamie, did you finish your homework last night?"

"Yes, ma'am."

Corra fixed her plate and sat at the table across from her kids. Together they ate breakfast like a normal family. The new normal for this Coleman family.

After breakfast Corra opened the front door to let the kids out so they could walk to the bus stop. Like little soldiers Jamie and Katie marched out onto the front porch with their backpacks on. Suddenly, they took off running down the steps yelling out, "Chris, Chris."

Corra stepped out the door as Chris came around the front of his car, smiling at the kids. Her pulse quickened as she yanked the headscarf from her hair and threw it behind the door. Chris gave Katie a hug, and Jamie a handshake. Her little man had grown up so much over the summer.

The school bus came screeching around the corner and the kids waved goodbye. Corra called after them to be good in school today.

As Chris strolled up the steps, she bit her lips to keep from smiling like a damned fool, but couldn't stop her heartbeat from racing.

"Good morning, Corra."

She crossed her arms. "Good morning." Chris looked ready for Wall Street instead of his small office in Danville. The butterflies started a dance in her stomach.

"The kids look good," he said, as he reached the porch.

"Thank you, they're excited about the new school year."

Chris nodded. "I hope you don't mind that I

stopped by. I, uh, thought maybe we could talk a minute."

She lowered her arms. "Sure, come on in. I've got a few minutes before I leave for work."

She closed the door behind them and followed him up into the living room.

"Corra, I've got something to say and I need you to listen."

She took a step back and looked up at him.

"Have a seat, please." He gestured toward her couch.

She crossed her arms.

"Sit down, Corra."

She didn't know what had got into him, but she walked over to the couch and sat down.

He let out a loud breath. "I've been agonizing over this for weeks. I made a mistake." He started pacing. "I've never dated a woman with children before, so this is all rather new for me. And I'm probably going to make more mistakes. But, I'm going to try like hell not to. All I know for sure is that I love you, and I want what we had back. I want you and the kids back in my life." He stopped pacing.

Corra lowered her head and closed her eyes to keep the tears from falling. Chris kneeled in front of her. He took her chin in his hand and raised it so they were eye to eye.

"What I'm asking is if we can start over? I told you before, you're the only one for me. I apologize for everything."

Corra smiled. "I accept your apology. And maybe

I overreacted a little too. The last couple of weeks have been crazy without having you to look forward to. You don't know how much I've missed you."

Chris stood up and pulled Corra into his arms. He kissed her. "Thank you. I've missed you too. And there's something else I've missed."

"What?"

He licked his lips and winked. "Well, we have the house to ourselves."

A shiver ran through her. "But don't you have to go to work?"

"I'm the boss. I can be late."

Corra smiled. "Yeah, I'm part owner. I can be late."

"You still got the Jimmy Choos?" he asked, arching a brow.

She reached down and took his hand. "Come on, let me show them to you."

Chris smiled and followed her upstairs to her bedroom.

* * * * *

SPECIAL EXCERPT FROM

Faith Alexander's guardian angel has a body built for sin. Ever since she woke up in the hospital after a car crash, her rescuer, Brandon Gray, has been by her side—chivalrous, caring and oh-so-fine. All Brandon's focus is on his long-coveted role as CEO—until he stops to help a mysterious beauty. With chemistry this irresistible, he's ready to share a future with Faith, but he feels beyond betrayed to discover what she's been hiding. If desire and trust can overcome pride, he'll realize he's found the perfect partner in the boardroom and the bedroom…

Read on for a sneak peek at
GIVING MY ALL TO YOU, the next exciting
installment in author Sheryl Lister's
***THE GRAYS OF LOS ANGELES** series!*

She frowned. *Who in the world…?* As if sensing her scrutiny, he opened his eyes and pushed up from the chair. Faith blinked. He was even taller than she originally thought, well-built and easily the most handsome man she'd seen in a long time.

"Hey," he said softly.

"I thought I dreamed you."

His deep chuckle filled the room. "No. I'm very real."

Faith tried to clear the cobwebs from her mind. "You helped me when I crashed." She thought for a moment. "Brandon?"

He nodded. "How are you feeling?"

"Everything hurts. Even breathing hurts." She closed her eyes briefly. "Um…what time is it?" she murmured.

Brandon checked his watch. "A little after eleven."

"You've been here all this time?"

"For the most part. I brought your stuff and I didn't want to leave it with anyone without your permission." He placed them on the tray.

"Thank you."

"Do you want me to call your husband or family?"

Faith wanted to roll her eyes at the husband reference, but just the thought made her ache, so she settled for saying "I'm not married."

"What about family—Mom, Dad?"

The last person she wanted to talk to was her mother. "My parents don't live here," she added softly. She had been on her way to her father's house, but chickened out before arriving and had turned around to go back to the hotel when she'd had the accident.

A frown creased his brow. "You don't have anyone here?"

"No. I live in Oregon. I just got here yesterday."

"Hell of a welcome."

"Tell me about it," she muttered.

"Well, now that I know you're okay, I'm going to leave. I'll stop by to see you tomorrow to make sure you don't need anything." Brandon covered her uninjured hand with his large one and gave it a gentle squeeze.

Despite every inch of her body aching, the warmth of his touch sent an entirely different sensation flowing through her. The intense way he was staring at her made her think he had felt something, as well.

"I…um…" Brandon eased his hand from hers. "Get some rest." However, he didn't move, his interest clear as glass. After another moment he walked to the door, but turned back once more. "Good night."

"Good night." Faith watched as he slipped out the door, her heart still racing. Her life seemed to be a mess right now, but knowing she would see Brandon again made her smile.

*Don't miss GIVING MY ALL TO YOU
by Sheryl Lister, available May 2017
wherever Harlequin® Kimani Romance™
books and ebooks are sold.*

Get 2 Free Books,
Plus 2 Free Gifts—
just for trying the Reader Service!

KROM17R